"Unforgettable . . . In this spellbinding, adrenaline-fueled debut linked collection, Mackin pulls from his own time in the Navy to follow a team of SEALs who, from 2008 to 2011, serve and try to survive together, primarily in Iraq and Afghanistan. Each story explodes with dust and dread. . . . It is the language as much as the experience that drives the action, creating taut, almost terrifying suspense. Mackin's masterful prose is both poetic and aggressive."   —*Publishers Weekly*, starred review

"Mackin turns in a virtuoso performance. . . . With vividly drawn characters and a strong sense of the absurdity of war, this striking debut collection will evoke memories of Tim O'Brien's classic Vietnam stories, *The Things They Carried*."
—*Booklist*

"Tobias Wolff once lamented that 'when people use the word "Nam" it's like salt on a slug.' But a recent spate of fiction about contemporary war (*Redeployment, Green on Blue*) signals an end to the combat clichés. Onto this fertile ground parachutes Will Mackin's *Bring Out the Dog*. A U.S. Navy veteran with five combat tours in Iraq and Afghanistan under his belt, Mackin also produces the kind of simultaneously sharp and ethereal writing that caused George Saunders to bless him with a story-length blurb. On one page of Mackin's debut are 'Taliban [leaping] from the ditch'; on the next, 'Time passed mysteriously inside the clouds.'"

—*Vanity Fair*

"*Bring Out the Dog* is not just one hell of a stunning debut—it's also proof that Mackin is one to watch going forward. Drawing from notes he took while working in special operations in Iraq and Afghanistan, the stories illuminate the human condition in unimaginable, haunting ways—and bring to life a voice that is unlike any other in the modern canon." —*PopSugar*

"[*Bring Out the Dog* is] blustery, unsettling, observant, absurd, and all too real." —*Fiction Advocate*

"Gritty, crisply written, cinematic stories."
—*Albuquerque Journal*

"Mackin has produced something that holds up alongside the very best war literature of the twenty-first century. . . . *Bring Out the Dog* is both complex and compelling, offering up small glimpses of the surreal alongside moments of heartbreak and of heroism. Mackin's prose displays a deftness that belies its basic muscularity; it's an ideal mix in terms of presenting these stories with the ring of genuine truth. . . . This is a brilliant debut, a work unafraid to use brute force to evoke an uncommon grace. Mackin's vision consummately captures the lives of soldiers dealing with the physical and psychological stresses of a seemingly unending war. Time will tell whether this book finds its spot among the best American creative works born of these wars, but from where I'm sitting, it'll be awfully difficult to deny *Bring Out the Dog* a place at that table. It is magnificent." —*The Maine Edge*

"The short book of short stories launches the twenty-three-year Navy veteran into the pantheon-in-progress of literary fiction coming out of today's wars." —*Military Times*

"Will Mackin's *Bring Out the Dog* . . . cuts through all the shiny and hyped-up rhetoric of wartime, and aggressively and masterfully draws a picture of the brutal, frightening, and even boring moments of deployment. . . . *The Things They Carried, Redeployment,* and now *Bring Out the Dog:* war stories for your bookshelf that will last a very long time, and serve as reminders of what America was, is, and can still become."

—*Chicago Review of Books*

"Every war seems to spawn its own bookshelf of fiction (e.g., Hemingway, Heller, O'Brien, Stone and, more recently, Klay, Powers and Ackerman), and the writers who endure display talents for observation, voice and narrative that outlive the high-strung emotion of the battlefield. A navy veteran with multiple deployments in Iraq and Afghanistan, Will Mackin is one of those with staying power. The stories in his debut, *Bring Out the Dog,* are told with such verisimilitude, such balance between compassion and cynicism, such lean haunting prose, that one can't easily shake them. . . . Read *Bring Out the Dog* for its insight into those who fight our modern wars, but read it again for its grasp of the vicissitudes of the human heart."

—*Shelf Awareness*

BRING
OUT
THE
DOG

BRING OUT THE DOG

STORIES

—

Will Mackin

RANDOM HOUSE

NEW YORK

2020 Random House Trade Paperback Edition

Published in the United States by Random House, an imprint and division of Penguin Random House LLC, New York.

RANDOM HOUSE and the HOUSE colophon are registered trademarks of Penguin Random House LLC.

Originally published in hardcover in the United States by Random House, an imprint and division of Penguin Random House LLC, in 2018.

"Kattekoppen," "Crossing the River No Name," and "The Lost Troop" were originally published in *The New Yorker*. Portions of "Great Circle Route Westward Through Perpetual Night" were originally published as "Dog" in *Diagram* 12.6. Portions of "Backmask" were originally published as "Dispatch 7: A Normal Human in the World" as part of a series entitled "Dispatches from Iraq" on *McSweeney's Internet Tendency* on October 5, 2007.

Library of Congress Cataloging-in-Publication Data
Names: Mackin, Will, author.
Title: Bring out the dog : stories / Will Mackin.
Description: First edition. | New York : Random House, 2018.
Identifiers: LCCN 2017027232| ISBN 9780812985689 |
ISBN 9780812995657 (ebook)
Subjects: | BISAC: FICTION / Short Stories (single author). |
FICTION / Literary. | FICTION / War & Military.
Classification: LCC PS3613.A27345 A6 2018 | DDC 813/.6—dc23
LC record available at lccn.loc.gov/2017027232

randomhousebooks.com

Book design by Victoria Wong

147028622

For Alaina, Betta, and Eli

We saw victory and defeat,
and they were both wonderful.

—Barry Hannah, "Midnight and
I'm Not Famous Yet"

Contents

———

BRING
OUT
THE
DOG

The Lost Troop

—

We had a dry spell in Logar. It was February, during which the weather was dog shit, so a degree of slowness was expected. But this went beyond slowness. It was like peace had broken out and nobody'd told us. Nights we'd meet in the OPS hut for the mission brief. We'd tune the flatscreens to the drones—over Ghazni, Orgun, and Khost—only to find all three orbiting within the same cloud. We'd listen to static on the UHF. We'd stare at phones that never rang. We might've left it all behind, walked off the outpost and into the desert, never to be seen again. We might've created the Legend of the Lost Troop. Rather, we chose someplace where we imagined the enemy might be hiding— a compound on the banks of the Helmand River, a brake shop in downtown Marjah, a cave high in the Hindu Kush— and we ventured out there, hoping for a fight.

I thought of the Japanese soldiers on Iwo Jima, who, when their island fell to the Americans, may not have known

that their island had fallen. Who, not long after, may not
have heard that A-bombs had destroyed Hiroshima and Na-
gasaki, and that their emperor had admitted defeat. Those
soldiers hid in tunnels on Iwo for weeks after the war was
over. For months, even. For them, the fight continued in those
dark and narrow spaces, until they ran out of food. Until
they drank the last of their water. Until, absent the means
and/or the will to take their own lives, they climbed out of
rat holes into the sun, to wander warm fields of lava rock, in
surrender.

I wondered what it would take for us. If, one night, we'd
drop out of the starry sky in our blacked-out helicopters near
a walled compound in the desert. We'd run toward that compound with the rotor wash at our backs, pushing us into the
dust cloud that had been kicked up by our arrival, and out
the other side. Passing through a crooked archway in the
compound's outer wall, we'd enter the courtyard. And there,
among the fig trees and goats, we'd find an American tourist
with a camera strapped around his neck.

Having served his time in Afghanistan, our fellow American had gone home, fallen in love, gotten married, and had
the two bow-headed daughters now hiding behind his legs.
Maybe he'd wanted his girls to see how brightly the stars
shone in the desert. Maybe he'd wanted to share with them
all the strange places the army had sent him, way back when.
I imagined that he'd look at us with understanding and re-
morse.

"Dudes, war's over."

But, as far as we knew, it wasn't. Therefore, we'd meet in the OPS hut every night at eight. In the absence of new intelligence, we'd review old intelligence. We'd double-check dead ends and reexamine cold cases. Finding nothing mission-worthy, Hal, our troop chief, would open the floor to suggestions. It'd be quiet for a while, as everyone thought.

"Come on," Hal would say.

He'd be standing in the middle of the plywood room. We'd be sitting on plywood tables, balancing on busted swivel chairs, leaning against the thin walls. Drones, orbiting inside moonlit thunderheads, would beam their emerald visions back to us. Lightning would strike twenty miles away and the UHF would crackle. I, for one, didn't have any good ideas to offer.

One night, Digger spoke up. "Who remembers that grave-yard decorated like a used-car lot, out in Khost?"

I raised my hand, along with a few others.

"I think we need to go back there," Digger said.

The graveyard in question was on the northern rim of a dusty crater. We'd patrolled past it, a few weeks prior, on an easterly course. The "used-car lot" decorations were plastic strands of multicolored pennants. One end of each strand was tied high in an ash tree that stood at the center of the graveyard. The other ends were staked into the hard ground outside the circle of graves. The graves themselves were piles of stones, shaped like overturned rowboats. I couldn't recall the name of our mission that night, its task and purpose, its outcome. But that graveyard stuck with me. I remembered the pennants snapping in the wind, dust parting around the graves like current.

Digger, who'd passed closer to the graveyard than I, thought the graves had looked suspicious. He believed they resembled old cellar doors. The type, I imagined, you'd find outside a farmhouse in Nebraska. The type you'd run to from darkened fields as a tornado was bearing down. Digger postulated that at least one of those graves was made of fake stones.

"Styrofoam balls," he suggested to us in the OPS hut, "painted to look like stones, then glued to a plywood sheet." Digger wondered if we might sneak into that graveyard, pull open this hypothetical door, descend a flight of stairs, and discover a Taliban nerve center, bomb factory, or armory. Digger had no idea what might be down there, but he'd gotten a weird feeling walking past that graveyard that night.

"Let's make it happen," Hal said.

We rode our helicopters—two dual-rotor, minigun-equipped MH-47s—southeast from Logar. We sat in mesh jump seats, across from one another, roughly ten per side. The MH-47, at altitude, stabilized like a swaying hammock. Its engines warbled like cop cars racing off to faraway trouble. Lube, dripping from the crankcase, smelled like bong water. At the back end of the tubular cargo bay, beyond the open ramp, night passed by like scenery in an old movie.

The 47s dropped us off in a dry riverbed, three miles west of the graveyard. We patrolled eastward under heavy clouds. The clouds carried a powerful static charge, while the earth remained neutral. Sparkling dust hovered, and my brothers, walking with me, appeared as concentrations of this dust. All I heard, as we walked, was my own breathing.

We connected with the crater's westernmost point, then walked in a clockwise direction along its rim until we reached the graveyard. We found the pennants torn and tattered; the ash tree diseased; the graves crooked. None of the stones were made of Styrofoam. Not one of the graves was an elaborately disguised entrance to a nefarious subterranean activity. Though, upon closer inspection, I noticed that the dust that I'd remembered parting around the graves, resembling current, actually funneled into the spaces between stones. In fact, the dust appeared to be getting sucked into those spaces. Which made it seem like there was some sort of void below the graves, creating a vacuum, and lent a measure of credence to Digger's theory.

From the top of one grave, I selected a smooth, round stone, about the size of a shot-put ball, and I heaved it into the crater.

Joe, our interpreter, was right there to scold me. "I would expect such disrespectful behavior from the Taliban," he said, "but not from you."

Joe was Afghani. His real name was Jamaluddein. Following the Soviet invasion of Afghanistan, in 1980, he'd escaped

to the U.K. with his parents. Joe was twelve years old at the
time. Now, as a middle-aged man, he'd returned to help save
his country from ruin. He wore armor on missions, but he
carried no weapons. His interpretations of our enemy's mut-
tered words were always clear and precise. He had a bad
habit of walking too close behind me on patrol, then closing
that distance whenever we made contact with the enemy.
Sometimes he'd bump into me and I'd turn around. Thus, I'd
seen conflagrations reflected in the smudged lenses of Joe's
glasses. I'd heard him whisper prayers between sporadic det-
onations. His voice, with its derived British accent and perpetual tone of disappointment, exactly matched that of my
beleaguered conscience.

So I jumped into the crater after the stone. I found it at the
end of a long, concave groove in the dust. Turning back
toward the crater's rim, I saw my bootprints descending the
slope, each as perfect as Neil Armstrong's first step on the
moon. On my way back up to the graveyard, I was careful
not to disturb those tracks, or the flawless groove that had
been carved by the stone. I wanted these things preserved, I
supposed, in the event that an asteroid should slam into the
planet, sloughing away the atmosphere, boiling the seas, and
ending life on earth in a matter of seconds.

Our troop—asphyxiated, desiccated, frozen—would lie
scattered about the graveyard, perfectly preserved in the
seamless void of space forever, or at least until other intelli-
gent beings came along and discovered us. Perhaps because

these beings existed as thin bars of blue light, incapable of offensive or defensive action, they'd puzzle over our armor, rifles, night-vision devices, and grenades. They'd wonder, especially, why we'd worn such things to a graveyard. There'd be no mystery, however, regarding the bootprints in the crater, since they'd know, by the boots still on my feet, that I'd been the one who'd left them. Furthermore, they'd deduce, by the groove, that I'd descended into the crater after a stone. Only one stone could've cut that groove. Thus, they'd find it among a thousand others, right where I'd returned it, atop the grave, just moments before the asteroid had struck the earth. But none of that would explain how the stone had wound up in the crater in the first place.

Had one of them thrown it? the curious bars of blue light might ask themselves.

The next night, in the OPS hut, we still had nothing, intelligence-wise. Hal asked for suggestions again. Another hush fell on the troop as we sat thinking. Hal stood in the middle of the plywood room. On the one hand, he loved the war. On the other, he loved us. Green clouds floated by on the flatscreens. Fuzzy static emanated from the UHF. Archie, who, a month prior, had replaced Yaz, who we'd lost in a soybean field in Konduz, stood up from the floor. He pulled a tin of breath mints from his shirt pocket.

"I probably should've told you guys about this sooner," he said.

The tin, Archie explained, had arrived in the mail about two weeks ago. It was sent by Yaz's widow, whose name was Connie.

I knew Connie from troop barbecues, Halloween parties, and the like. I remembered her, once, dressed as a cowgirl and dancing in Digger's kitchen. She fired cap guns at the ceiling, which made the fluorescent light hazy. Yaz, standing by the bean dip, watched his wife holster her toy pistols. He smiled as she spun an invisible lasso over her head. Roping Yaz, Connie pulled him in, hand over hand, while Yaz feigned resistance. His breath must've smelled like corn chips. Hers, I imagined, smelled just fine.

The tin Archie showed us in the OPS hut contained a handful of Yaz's ashes.

"Connie asked me to find a good place to spread these around," he said. "And I tried, but no place seems good enough. You guys got any ideas?"

Digger suggested that we climb to the top of Mount Noshack—i.e., the tallest peak in Afghanistan—and release Yaz's ashes into a spindrift. Tull proposed a verdant meadow, north of J-bad, where he and Yaz once went AWOL to hunt elk. I made an argument for the tiny garden of purple flowers that had grown behind Yaz's tent, where he used to spit out his toothpaste. Hal, however, wanted to return to Konduz.

Konduz was four hundred kilometers north of Logar. The 47s flew higher than usual to get there. Frost formed on the cargo bay's circular windows. The engines whined, the rotors slipped, and the helicopter wobbled as if we were balancing at the end of a very long pole. I almost hoped that something would go wrong. Nothing catastrophic, of course. Just a low-oil light or engine temperature creeping into the red. Something that would force us to land short and reconsider. I didn't want to see that field again, in Konduz, with its dark puddles reflecting the stars, with its soybean shoots glowing white. I didn't want to smell its fertilized tang. But nothing went wrong. We touched down on the western edge of the field, right where we'd touched down before, opposite the ditch that had given me so much trouble.

We'd first landed in that field on a clear night in late December. Jupiter had been the focal point of a crescent moon. The ditch where we knew the enemy was hiding was east of our position, and outside of small-arms range. I thought, at the time, that there were no more than a half dozen Taliban in that ditch. I'd based that estimate, partly, on how the shrubbery had quaked when they'd scurried around behind it. I'd considered, as well, the frequency of AK fire, which, from that safe distance, sounded like movie projectors running out of film. I'd seen and heard these things before. For six Taliban wallowing in a muddy ditch, I figured that a pair of thousand-pound bombs, with delayed fuses, ought to do the trick.

A combination of ash and sissoo trees stood in that ditch. Shrubbery tangled the spaces between those trees. I brought two jets in from the north, in trail formation. The first bomb ignited every tree and shrub. The second launched their burning trunks like moon shots. I turned to my right, expecting to find Hal. Instead, I found Joe—hands in pockets, armored belly protruding. The burning trench was reflected in his dirty glasses.

Hal appeared from behind me. "You done?" he asked.

What remained of the shrubbery was still, and the AKs had fallen silent.

"Yes," I said.

We spread ourselves the length of the field for mop-up, then walked toward the ditch in a line abreast. Stars jiggled in puddles. The mud smelled like turpentine. Soybean shoots resembled those albino creatures that lived in the Atlantic's deepest trench. Hal walked next to me. Yaz walked five men past Hal. The machine gun Yaz carried weighed as much as the front axle on a Sentra. Its rounds were the size of soup cans. As we stepped into small-arms range, Tull whistled like a bird, in warning. A Taliban popped out of the ditch seconds later. The barrel of his AK, we believed, was bent. The majority of his volley curved skyward.

More Taliban leapt from the ditch after Yaz fell. Dozens, in fact. We turned them around quick enough; then we fell back, dragging Yaz. Joe was right behind me, breathing hard. Hal called for CASEVAC even though Yaz was already dead. Maybe he didn't want us thinking that he wouldn't do the same thing for us. Maybe he wanted to give us one more reason to believe that he'd never give up. Or maybe he just wanted us to fight and not worry about it.

I called out to every jet in the sky. The first wave arrived just as the CASEVAC was lifting off with Yaz. I brought the jets down in a clockwise spiral. I had them toss everything they had—five-hundred-, one-thousand-, two-thousand-pounders—into the ditch. A second wave of jets joined the first in the spiral, then a third, and a fourth. I bombed the ditch until the mud puddles in the soybean field steamed, until the soybean shoots themselves melted, until it seemed as though I were standing in the ditch and bombing the field.

That soybean field looked no different in February. The ditch was unchanged, too, although some of the trees and shrubbery were gone. I stood in the same place I'd stood while controlling the jets, back in December. The rest of the troop walked into the field behind Archie. They formed a circle around him at the spot where Yaz was killed. Archie took a knee and pulled the tin from his pocket. He opened the lid and tapped the side of the tin with his finger. I didn't want to see the ashes fall, so I turned around, and there was Joe.

"It wasn't your fault," he said.

TIME PASSED MYSTERIOUSLY inside the clouds. Unlike when the orbiting drones could see the ground, and a haystack or a cow would spin around on the flatscreens like a second hand, we sat watching the spinning clouds without knowing for how long. Meanwhile, the UHF clicked like something radioactive. This was the night after Konduz, or the night after our return to Konduz. We had no intelligence, still. Sitting cross-legged on the floor, I tried peace on for size. I felt proud that I'd fought, or something like proud, but also glad it was over. Hal asked for suggestions, and Joe raised his hand.

Hal said, "You don't need to raise your hand."

"I had a teacher, in primary school, who used to hit my knuckles with a ruler," Joe said. "I would like to pay him a visit."

"I had a teacher like that," Hal said.

"Me, too," Digger said.

The rest of us nodded, remembering.

Joe had last seen his teacher at his old school, in the town of Ghawas, in Wardak Province, in 1979. Joe had been eleven at the time. The teacher had seemed ancient to Joe back then. In hindsight, however, Joe figured that his teacher had been no older than thirty. Which meant that there was a good chance, in 2009, that the teacher was still alive. He'd lived in a cabin near a forest, Joe remembered, though he couldn't say exactly where. Joe assured us, though, that he could find the cabin if we could find his old school.

We'd never had reason to patrol through Ghawas; therefore, we had no maps of tactical value. Digger, who always planned our routes, turned to the computer that contained the satellite imagery. Our imagery of Ghawas was both stale and irregular. Half of it dated from the winter of 2003, the other half from the spring of 2005. The school, Joe said, was a stone building on the eastern bank of a river. It had stood just north of a bend in the river that was shaped like a question mark.

Hal, Joe, and I stood behind Digger as he searched Ghawas for a river with a question mark. He found it in an image that had been captured by a satellite on a May afternoon in 2005. Digger zoomed in, and we saw the river's banks overflowing with snowmelt. Sunlight sparkled in the eddies. Reeds grew from stagnant pools. Digger scrolled northbound in search of the school. The imagery changed to winter, 2003. The river narrowed and turned dark as slate. A hundred yards north of the question mark, on the river's eastern bank, we discovered a stone foundation poking from the ice. Joe thought it was too small to be the ruins of his old school, but then he realized it had to be.

From the school's foundation, Joe guided Digger along the path the teacher had walked on his way home. It ran north along the river for a snowy mile; then the imagery switched back to spring, and the path cut east into a warm field of grass. As a student, Joe used to follow the teacher at a safe distance across this field. Crouching in the tall grass, he would fantasize about leaping out and knocking his teacher down. More than revenge, though, he'd wanted to study his teacher. He'd kept his eyes on his desk in class all day, hoping to stay out of trouble. Following the teacher home was Joe's chance to finally see the man. Joe described his teacher as tall and prematurely gaunt. He said that the teacher had worn a heavy robe during his walks home in winter. He remembered butterflies rising in the teacher's wake when he crossed the grassy field in spring.

"Keep going," Joe said to Digger.

Digger continued scrolling across the sunlit field to a snow-covered forest. The image of that forest had been captured on a January evening in 2003. Shadows cast by the tall, bare trees looked like minute hands, all showing ten past the hour. Halfway across the forest, the satellite imagery ran out. The computer screen turned black.

"He lives on the other side of that forest," Joe said.

"How far?" Hal asked.

Joe touched a spot on the dark computer screen. "Here."

The four of us looked at that spot.

"I'm thinking callout," Digger said to Hal.

Callouts were best in unknown situations. Like, we didn't know whether or not the cabin existed or, if it did, how big it might be. We didn't know who, other than the teacher, might be hiding inside or how prepared they might be to mount a defense. To mitigate the risks posed by these unknowns, a callout would proceed in stages. The 47s would drop us off outside the cabin, beyond small-arms range. If we took fire from the cabin, we'd keep our distance, and I'd call in an air strike. If not, we'd run toward the cabin, then surround it on two sides. Digger would throw a flash bang through a window. Light would tear through the cabin. Bangs would echo in the night. After all was dark and quiet, Joe would read a statement into a bullhorn, informing the startled occupants that we were coalition forces, there to protect the rights of the Afghan people.

"Yeah," Hal said. "Let's go with a callout. But no flash bang. And Joe, I want you to say something different tonight."

Hal chose a line from the end of a song by Pink Floyd called "Another Brick in the Wall (Part 2)." The song opens with the lyric "We don't need no education" and goes on to denounce teachers as repressive and cynical. The song ends in a riot. As the students tear down their school, a teacher's voice can be heard above the din. He's hollering admonishments, such as "Wrong! Do it again!" and "Stand still, laddie!" Hal chose one such rebuke for Joe to shout through the bullhorn. Joe practiced it on the helicopter ride out to Ghawas.

" 'If you don't eat your meat, you can't have any pudding . . . ' "

"No," Hal interrupted. "You need more fear in your voice."

Joe and Digger sat on one side of the helicopter, Hal and I on the other. Night parted around us and mended in our wake.

"I don't think 'fear' is the right word," I said.

"It's Joe's teacher," Digger said. "Let him say it however he wants."

"The teacher in the song is staring down an angry mob," Hal said. "He can't just say the words."

"I think my teacher is more crazy than afraid," Joe said.

"All right," Hal said. "Let's hear it again."

The windows in the MH-47 were made of Plexiglas. They were shaped like mixing bowls. Looking through them, I saw things on the outside as either close and blurry, or far away and blurry. There was a sweet spot in the lens, however, where something would emerge perfectly magnified. Thus, when we banked over the highway that ran between Kandahar and Kabul, I saw a bleary-eyed trucker behind the wheel. When we floated over the mountains into Wardak, I saw a waterfall cascading into a crystalline lake. And when we turned above the ruins of Joe's old school, I imagined the school as it had once been—stone walls, slate roof, and leaded glass windows.

We cut across the field of tall grass and sped over the woods at treetop level. The rotors beat louder as we pulled into a hover. We touched down on either side of the teacher's cabin, without taking fire. The 47s lifted off behind us as we ran. Rotor wash shoved me through clumps of dry grass and over the tops of warm, surfacing boulders. Archie, carrying Yaz's massive gun, ran ahead of me, while Joe, carrying his red bullhorn, ran behind. The teacher's cabin was made of logs. Grass grew on the roof. A curl of smoke rose from its stone chimney. A neatly stacked woodpile stood behind it. Empty rabbit traps leaned against a wall. We formed lines on two sides of the cabin. Taking position next to Hal, I saw myself reflected in a dark blue window.

We stood, still and quiet, outside the teacher's cabin as the 47s descended into a valley. Soon enough, their noise became a memory; then that memory faded. A cold wind rustled the grass. Our breath rose in thick clouds. I imagined the teacher lying awake in bed, wondering if he'd only dreamed of helicopters landing outside.

Hal nodded at Joe, and Joe raised his bullhorn.

" 'If you don't eat your meat, you can't have any pudding! *How* can you have any pudding if you don't eat your meat!' "

Joe's message echoed. A match flared inside the cabin, turning the windows orange. The teacher emerged in a nightcap, carrying a lit candle on a brass candlestick. He squinted at us standing in the darkness.

Digger slapped away the candle. Hal stepped on the flame. I zip-tied the old man's wrists, and Joe forced him to kneel on the hard ground.

"What have I done?" he asked.

We didn't answer. Rather, we left him, knees bleeding, to think about it. Then we burst into his cabin to see how he lived.

Welcome Man Will Never Fly

Dare County, North Carolina

Rain soaked the flatbed. It drummed off the deuce-and-a-half's rusty cab. It ran down the sides of the blue shipping container—half-sunk in the marsh, 150 meters south of our position—that was our target on that December evening in 2008. Moby was on the radio, running the control. Reed and I were both JTACs, or joint terminal attack controllers, or those who, from the ground, directed air attacks against the enemy. We were training Moby to be a JTAC too, but it wasn't going well. Only one of the four jets that we'd scheduled had shown up. Then the storm had blown in. And now the sun had gone down, leaving the sky to the west—in which we searched for the jet—dark gray.

"Got him," Reed said.

"Where?" Moby asked.

Reed pointed. "Right there, turning in."

Moby shook his head.

"Out over the Alligator River," I added.

"That doesn't help," Moby said.

The jet—a Hornet, call sign "Ripper"—appeared low over the trees, turning hard toward the range, its wings wrapped in a bright cloud of white vapor. Rolling out of the turn with its nose pointed at us, the jet became invisible.

"Ripper, inbound, heading one-zero-three," the pilot radioed. I thought his voice sounded familiar.

"What do I tell him?" Moby asked.

"Do you have him in sight?" Reed asked.

"No."

"Then say 'Continue' and keep looking."

A gust of wind sharpened the rain at our backs. Moby held the radio's hook like a phone as he keyed the mike. After five seconds of dead air, he said, "Continue."

Navy Dare Bombing Range was at the center of a wide, brackish marsh. At the western end of that marsh, roughly three miles from the flatbed, stood a forest of tall pines. Beyond the pines was the Alligator River, so called because that's what everyone thought it looked like from the air. But I'd flown over that river dozens of times, and I'd never seen the alligator.

Before becoming a JTAC, in 2004, I was a pilot, which was all I'd ever wanted to be. I'd joined the navy wanting to fly the F-14 Tomcat, like Maverick in *Top Gun*. I'd dreamed of speeding into dogfights at Mach 1. After flight school, however, I was assigned to fly a subsonic monstrosity known as the Queer. The Queer was a Vietnam-era bomber that had, as a bombsight, grease-pencil crosshairs on the windscreen. Every now and then I used to fly a Queer to Navy Dare, to work with SEAL JTACs. Approaching the range from the west, I'd look down on the river and try to see the alligator. Its jaws, I'd heard, opened north; its tail curved south; tributaries formed its legs. I didn't see any of that. At the center of the river was a star-shaped island that was supposed to be the gator's eye. I'd begin my target runs over that island, heading east-southeast toward a dead cypress that stood taller than all the pines.

I elbowed Moby and pointed at the cypress. "Ripper's over that dead tree now," I said.

"There's, like, a million fucking dead trees," Moby said.

Ripper approached the target at over five hundred knots. Vapes thick as whipped cream flashed on the backs of his wings.

"Okay, now I see him," Moby said.

"Clear him hot," Reed said.

"*Ripper, two miles,*" the pilot said. He could've been Biff, who I'd known in flight school.

"What the fuck's he talking about, two miles?" Moby asked.

"He wants clearance," I said.

Ripper disappeared into a thick, dark squall, the type I would've avoided at all costs because the Queer's engines had a tendency to flame out in heavy precipitation. Something about the shape of the intakes allowed too much water to pass into the compressor, which then sprayed it all into the burner cans. But the Hornet had better intakes, apparently, along with better everything else. Ripper popped out of the squall unscathed.

"Clear him," Reed told Moby.

Moby palmed the big green radio in his left hand while holding the hook to his ear with his right. He keyed the mike and froze. Sometimes, as soon as he remembered what to say, he'd unfreeze. But this time Moby remained frozen. He stared off the flatbed into a murky rush of sawgrass with his mouth hanging open and rain dripping off his chin. My hypothesis was that the ten watts radiating off the transmitter triggered a petit mal in Moby's brain. I imagined the tight waves of radio energy penetrating Moby's skull and short-circuiting his thoughts. Then again, it didn't happen every time. Just often enough to cast doubt on his ability to control air strikes in a combat situation, which was more than enough to jeopardize the plan.

The plan was for Moby, a SEAL with Team Four, to replace Reed at the top secret unit to which Reed and I belonged. Moby wanted to leave Team Four because, according to him, they didn't deploy enough. Reed wanted to leave our unit because we deployed all the time, and he was burned out. Over five years, in fact, Reed had made seven deployments, plus however many contingency ops—including that last one, in Yemen, that had gone sideways. In order for Reed to leave, though, he needed to find his own replacement, i.e.

Moby, then train and qualify him as a JTAC. And he needed to do it before Christmas, because that's when Reed's troop was scheduled to deploy again.

Moby failed to transmit clearance. Ripper passed low over the shipping container without dropping any of its inert training bombs. The noise of the Hornet's engines at full power sounded like everything in the world being torn apart. I followed Ripper's ascent into the clouds via its anti-collision light, which made those clouds blink red. Reed followed, too. Moby turned up the volume on the radio to hear the pilot say, "Ripper's off target, no drop, RTB."

RTB meant "return to base."

"I guess we're done," Moby said.

"Gimme that," I said.

Moby passed me the hook. "Is this Biff?" I transmitted.

Last I'd heard, Biff was flying Hornets on the West Coast, though he could've been transferred.

"Negative. This is Keebler," the pilot radioed back.

"Listen, Keebler. We need more passes."

"No can do," Keebler said. "There's a large cell of convective activity moving in. If I were you, I'd seek immediate shelter."

THE M35 TWO-AND-A-HALF-TON flatbed, a.k.a. the "deuce-and-a-half," was, like the Queer, a piece of Cold War equipment that had been nursed along for decades. At some point, this one had been farmed out to Navy Dare, where all nursing stopped. Where everything eventually got sucked into the marsh to decompose. The deuce-and-a-half's windshield was cracked, its clutch burned out. Its dim headlights surged whenever the worn-out alternator belt found purchase. A hole in the exhaust pipe pumped carbon monoxide into the cab. Reed rode shotgun with the window down. Moby rode bitch. I drove over washed-out dirt roads, through a thunderstorm, toward the control tower.

Moby pinched his nose to make his voice sound like Keebler's. "I advise you to seek immediate shelter," he said. "There's a large convention of dorks moving in."

I remembered looking down on a thunderstorm at night, from my perch in the Queer, seeing green lighting shudder in an anvil cloud, watching blue streaks of hail shoot out of the top.

A clear bolt of lightning tore the dark sky in half.

"Keebler was right, though," I said.

"That's the problem with you pilots," Moby said. "You're wrapped too goddamn tight."

SEALs had their own problems, but being uptight wasn't one of them. If anything, they'd gone too far in the opposite direction.

"Like, why can't you just sign me off?" Moby asked.

I rolled into a muddy pond in third gear without saying a word. Cold water seeped up through the perforated floorboards. Moby was asking me to forge his paperwork, to make him a JTAC without having him jump through the requisite hoops. Which I probably could've done, and nobody would've cared. But this was Reed's question to answer, not mine, because if Moby failed to qualify then Reed would have to deploy again. And it was Reed, not me, who was haunted by that contingency op back in Yemen, which had gone so wrong back in October. Reed and I were brothers—by fire, not blood—and I only wanted what was best for him. If that meant working overtime to get Moby legally qualified, then so be it. And if that meant forging the paperwork to give Moby a qualification that he didn't earn, well, then, so be that, too. The muddy water had risen above my boots. Feeling my way through a downshift, I dug out of the pond in second gear.

"You gotta do the whole JTAC syllabus," Reed said. "Start to finish."

"Like we have time for that," Moby said.

"Stranger things have happened," Reed said.

"What if I asked Jimmy to sign me off? You think he'd do it?"

Jimmy was a SEAL, too, and the leader of Three Troop, to which Reed was assigned. Jimmy was also the Hero of the Battle of Koshwan Ghar.

"Jimmy can do whatever the fuck he wants," Reed said.

THE CONTROL TOWER, with its faded red-and-white checkerboard paint job, appeared in the headlights. Its entrance was boarded up. Rainwater gushed from a broken drainpipe.

I parked the deuce-and-a-half at the base of the tower, and left the keys in the driver's-side visor. We transferred all our gear—radios, compasses, laser range finders, et cetera—into the Suburban, which was brand-new, bone-dry, and smelled like leather. Its high beams obliterated the rain, and I could barely hear the thunder from inside. I drove east off the range and took a left onto 264—a wide, freshly paved highway, with deep woods on either side. As I navigated the highway's gentle curves through the storm, Reed and Moby fell asleep.

It was two and a half hours back to our compound in Virginia, which would've put us there around ten. Normally, at that hour, the parking lot would be empty. But it would be even more so at this time of year, under holiday routine, with both the SCIF and the armory closed. The only car that would be in the lot, then, was Jimmy's jet-black 1972 Lincoln Continental—with its fastback, vinyl roof, and 460 V-8; with its peekaboo headlights and hood ornament like the cross-hairs off a Soviet anti-aircraft gun. Jimmy had no wife, no kids, and no life outside our covert band of hooligans. Some said Jimmy owned a mansion out in Hilltop, with teak-wood floors, granite countertops, and an infinity pool; but for all practical purposes, Jimmy lived on the compound, in a tin shack behind the dive locker, behind the paraloft, and be-hind the kill house where we practiced our assaults. I'd find Jimmy in that shack, on the couch, possibly hammered, watching TV.

Jimmy loved this twenty-four-hour network that showed

nothing but soaps, which, personally, I couldn't abide. Watching the same two impossibly attractive people face off in the same dimly lit, overdecorated rooms, in order to hash out the same old ridiculous problems, day after day, seemed to me a waste of time. Honestly, I equated such behavior with weakness. But that was hard to reconcile in Jimmy's case.

The Battle of Koshwan Ghar had taken place at the top of an eleven-thousand-foot mountain, in two feet of snow, back when the war was young. A drone had recorded the action via its infrared camera, and I'd watched the playback many times over the years, either as part of the viewing audience during the official commemoration on the anniversary of the battle, or alone at my desk on any given morning.

Hot is black in the video, and Jimmy's thermal signature is the blackest thing onscreen. Blacker than the exposed slabs of granite that had spent all day absorbing the sun's rays. Blacker than the muzzle flash of the Taliban's PKM. And blacker than Jimmy's pinned-down troopmates. Jimmy maneuvers under fire to take cover behind a petrified mulberry tree whose trunk immediately bursts into splinters. From there, Jimmy sprints toward the PKM itself, taking three spectacular strides before he gets hit in the leg, rolls in the snow, pops up, then proceeds to give the Taliban the good news. That was Jimmy's term for it, anyway, repurposed from the gospel. I didn't know if I'd ever find redemption, but watching that video of Jimmy on Koshwan Ghar seemed pretty damn close. And rewatching it every so often was my version of going to church.

Highway 264 ended at a T-intersection with a blinking yellow light. I took a right, rolled downhill into Manns Harbor, then across a low, concrete bridge with rhythmic tar seams. The water on either side churned like Hokusai's *The Great Wave*, with peaks rising over the bridge and halfway up the lampposts. Reed slept up front and Moby snored in back as we rolled off the bridge onto Bodie Island, where I took a left at a four-way intersection with a dark traffic light. The road would carry us north past Kill Devil Hills and the Wright Brothers' monument, past the home of Grave Digger, the famous monster truck, and into Virginia. My plan was to drop Moby off at his shithole in Pungo, and Reed at his apartment in Princess Anne, before driving to the compound at Dam Neck. I'd park next to Jimmy's magnificent Lincoln, then walk in the rain past the paraloft and the kill house to the dive locker. Golden light would shine out the seams of Jimmy's tin shack, nestled in the sand dunes.

Driving north through sea spray, past boarded-up strip malls and wobbly stop signs, I imagined the conversation that would take place between Jimmy and me.

"Now, who's this guy?" Jimmy would ask from the couch.

I'd be standing on the rug by the TV. "Moby," I'd say. "He's from Team Four."

"And what's his fuckin' problem?"

"He doesn't have the aptitude to be a JTAC. I'm sure he'll make a great assaulter, but . . ."

"What do you know about being an assaulter?" Jimmy would ask, staring.

The TV, on mute, would be showing a rerun of *One Life to Live*. Specifically, that epic scene where Real Bo returns from Parts Unknown to confront Fake Bo.

"And why can't Reed deploy?" Jimmy would ask.

"He's done, mentally," I'd say. "Those cluster-bombed kids in Yemen really messed him up."

"And you're still with One Troop?"

"Yeah."

"I could talk to Hal. Bring you over."

Hal, the leader of One Troop, was another hero, with another story.

"I'd rather not get in the middle of that," I'd say.

My attention returned to the road. Up ahead, I saw flashing lights. A little closer, cops appeared in shiny raincoats, sparking flares. A giant section of the road had been washed out by the storm. I turned around and went the other way, hoping to find a hotel.

THE UNLIT SIGN out in front of the hotel read, WELCOME MAN WILL NEVER FLY. The parking lot was full of cars. Wind ripped off the ocean, around the building, and stung my face. Inside, the lobby was dark, the front desk vacant. There was no BE BACK SOON sign, no bell to ring.

"Hello!" I yelled.

"I'll go find someone," Moby said.

As soon as he was gone, Reed said, "That guy's a piece of work."

"Yup," I said.

The two of us dripped on the carpet.

"I can't do another deployment, man. I just can't."

"I know," I said.

"Maybe we can line something up at Dare for next week. Bring in some Strike Eagles from Andrews, some Harriers from Cherry Point. We could get Moby, like, a hundred controls in a day."

"It's worth a try," I said, knowing full well that nobody was going to sign up for anything this close to Christmas.

Moby returned, followed by an old man in a tuxedo.

"This guy's Amish or something," Moby said.

The old man carried a tumbler of what looked like bourbon. He wore a small tux with a crooked bow tie. He smiled at us.

"You got any rooms?" Reed asked.

The old man shrugged. "I don't work here," he said.

Moby reached over the front desk and picked up a phone. "Hello?" he said. "Anybody out there?"

"So," the old man said. "I hear you're Marcinko's boys."

Commander Richard Marcinko, U.S. Navy, retired, was the founder of our little top secret unit.

"What'd you tell him?" Reed asked Moby.

Behind the front desk now, Moby was flipping light switches, jiggling mice. "I told him the truth. Sue me," Moby said.

"My name's John," said the man in the tux. "I worked with Dick Marcinko back in sixty-eight, in Laos. He called me in on slopes humping the Ho Chi Minh Trail, and I dropped beehives on them from my F-4."

Beehives were, like, poison dart bombs. They were banned by the Geneva Convention.

I pointed at John's tux. "What's the occasion?" I asked.

"I'm president of the Man Will Never Fly society. All of us are what you'd call pilots, or former pilots. We get together every year, on the anniversary of the Wright Brothers' imaginary achievement, to celebrate the myth of man-made flight."

"But you flew the F-4," Reed said.

"That's what they tell me," John said.

"I used to fly Queers," I said.

"I'm sorry to hear that," John said.

A hotel employee appeared, wearing a flowered vest that matched the lobby's carpet. He was soaked. "We almost have the generator online, sir," he said to John.

"Wonderful," John said. "How much longer?"

"Just a few minutes."

John opened his arms wide and a little booze sloshed out of his glass. The way he closed his eyes and inhaled, I thought he was going to break into song. Instead, he asked, "Would you gentlemen do me the honor of joining us for dinner?"

We followed John down an emergency-lit corridor toward the hotel ballroom.

"What about hot air balloons?" Reed asked.

"I believe in hot air," John said.

"And birds?" Moby asked.

"Birds are not men."

John stopped us before a crack in an accordion partition, on the other side of which was the ballroom. Through the crack I could see candles burning. I could hear voices and laughter.

"These people you're about to meet," John whispered. "They all look fine, but there's something wrong with them. You could say I was put in charge to keep an eye on things."

John opened a wider space in the partition, waving Reed and Moby through. He touched a finger to my chest to stop me from following.

"How long has it been since your last flight?" John whispered. His breath smelled like fuel.

"Six years," I said.

"Have you had that dream yet where you've forgotten how to land?"

"No," I said.

John looked toward the red exit sign at the far end of the hall. "Well, that'll come," he said.

Inside the ballroom, dozens of well-dressed couples sat at however many candlelit tables. Tiny flames turned their faces orange.

"What's the good word?" a round-faced man shouted at John.

"That knucklehead's an astronaut," John said to us, and everybody laughed.

"Who are your friends?" asked a lady in a red dress.

"Patience," John said.

The ocean sprayed against the picture windows that reflected the candlelit ballroom. We followed John to the center of the tables, where he stopped.

"Comrades," John said. "I was told, just a few minutes ago, that power would be restored in a few minutes. And . . ." He snapped his fingers. "Something else . . ."

"Your *friends*!" said the lady in the red dress.

"Of course," John said. "How could I forget our honored guests, who believe in flying machines, but we won't hold that against them."

"Bullshit!" the astronaut yelled.

"Bullshit, indeed," John said. "But they are otherwise fine, upstanding young men."

Waves crashed outside, threatening to shatter the picture windows. Reed, Moby, and I stood with our arms crossed in the dark.

"You'll see for yourselves in just a minute," John said.

Kattekoppen

———

Logar, Afghanistan

We went through a number of howitzer liaisons before Levi. His predecessors, none of whose names I remember, were able to build artillery plans in support of our night raids. They were skilled enough to communicate these plans to the soldiers who would fire the howitzers. In fact, any one of them would've been perfectly fine as a liaison to a normal organization. But ours was not a normal organization. Sometimes what went on gave normal men pause. And if they paused, we'd send them back and demand a replacement. After a few rounds of this, the lieutenant in charge of the howitzer battery said, "Enough."

Which was understandable, but not acceptable. So, on our first night without a mission, Hal and I took a walk to the howitzer camp. We set out from the dog cages under a full moon, which seemed to cast X-rays rather than light. Thus, the dogs' ribs were exposed, as was the darkness below the ice on our steep climb uphill. The steel barrels of the howitzer guns were visible as shadows, and the plywood door of the howitzer camp was illuminated as if it were bone. Hal knocked on the door with an ungloved fist.

The lieutenant answered. "Hey, guys," he said.

Hal pushed past him into the empty room. "Get your men in here," he said.

The room filled with soldiers feigning indifference, but every one of them had ideas about the war. The variety of ideas among soldiers developed into a variety of ideas among units, which necessitated an operational priority scheme. As SEAL Team Six, we were at the top of that scheme. Our ideas about the war *were* the war. Therefore, we could knock on any unit's door in the middle of the night, assemble the soldiers in a room, and tell them what was what.

On this night, Hal told them that we needed a goddamn liaison. Then he scanned the room for one. Levi's height—he was by far the tallest man there—made it easy for Hal to point and say, "How about you?"

You put a normal man on the spot like that and he'll get this look. Levi did not get that look. This may have been, at least partly, because Levi was Dutch, born and raised. Why he had joined the United States Army was anyone's guess.

"Yes," Levi answered. "I am available. Howeffer, I have a pregnant wife in Texas, and in two weeks' time I would like to go there for the burt of my son."

Hal, with his scar like a frown even when he was smiling, nodded my way. I nodded back.

"We can work that out," Hal said.

LEVI BECAME OUR howitzer liaison. He moved into our compound and had his mail delivered to our tactical operations center. Every now and then, packages would arrive from his mother in Amsterdam. Inside the packages was a variety of Dutch candy.

Levi opened these packages at his desk. He removed the *ouwels* and the *stroopwafels* and kept them for himself, but he always left the Kattekoppen in the box. Apparently, Levi had loved these candies as a kid, and his mother was under the impression that he still loved them. But he didn't. He set the Kattekoppen on the shelf by the door, where we kept boxes of unwanted food.

Perhaps "unwanted" is too strong a word. Better to say, maybe, that no one wanted that particular type of food at that particular time. Everyone knew, however, that a time would come, born of boredom, curiosity, or need, when we would want some Carb Boom, squirrel jerky, or a Clue bar. But until that time, the food sat on the shelf. And Kattekoppen sat longer than most.

American licorice was red or black. It came in ropes or tubes. Kattekoppen were neither black nor red. They were brown cat heads with bewildered faces. They made me think of a bombing attack I'd been involved in, in Helmand, during a previous deployment. We'd dropped a five-hundred-pound laser-guided bomb with a delayed fuse on a group of men standing in a circle in a dusty field. The round hit at the center of the circle and buried itself, by design, before the fuse triggered the explosion. The blast killed the men instantly, crushing their hearts and bursting their lungs, then flung their bodies radially. The dead landed on their backs, and a wave of rock and dirt, loosed by the explosion, sailed over them. The dust, however, floated above.

As we walked in from our covered positions, the dust descended slowly. By the time we reached the impact site, it had settled evenly on the dead, shrouding their open eyes and filling their open mouths. Those dusty faces, their uniform expressions of astonishment, were what I thought of when I saw Kattekoppen.

Nevertheless, the day came when I pulled a Kattekoppen out of the bag and held it up.

"How's this taste?" I asked Levi.

"Goot," he said.

I popped the cat head into my mouth and chewed, and I found that it did not taste goot. In fact, it tasted like ammonia. I ran outside and spat the chewed-up bits on the snow, but the bad taste remained. Thinking that snow might help, I ate some. When that failed, I chewed on some pine needles. But nothing worked.

Others who tried Kattekoppen didn't even make it outside. They simply spat their vociferous and obscene rejections right into the trash can next to Levi's desk. If these rebukes of his childhood favorite bothered Levi, he never let on. He just sat in his little chair, which was actually a normal chair dwarfed by his abnormal size, and, with his wee M16 by his side, he drew circles.

In a perfect world, there would be no circles. There would be two points, launch and impact, and between them a flawless arc. But in reality, our maps were best guesses, the winds erratic, and every howitzer barrel idiosyncratically bent. Not to mention the imperfect men who operated the howitzers—those who lifted the shells into the breech, who loaded the charges, who programmed the fuses. These men were exhausted, lonesome, and fallible.

Levi's circles were graphic depictions of possible error. They described—given the dry weight of a shell and the power of its propellant charge—where the howitzer rounds might fall. He drew them around our most likely targets, and since everything was always subject to change, he did so in grease pencil on a laminated map. Every circle contained a potential target, along with a subset of Afghanistan proper, its wild dogs, hobbled goats, ruined castles, and winter stars.

Before a mission, I'd study Levi's map. I'd follow the chain of circles along our patrol route. Within those circles, I'd trace the map's contour lines, to understand the rise and fall of the terrain. Thus I'd know fingers from draws, hills from craters. I could picture an attack in each place, the flashes of light, the rising columns of dust. Similarly, I'd study the stamps on the packages sent by Levi's mother.

These stamps paid tribute to the painter Brueghel. Each stamp focused on a particular detail within a particular painting. For example, the image on the stamp featuring *Hunters in the Snow* was of the hunters and their dogs returning from the hunt. Staggering through knee-deep drifts, they crested a hill that overlooked their tiny village.

Returning from our manhunts through the snowy mountains west of Logar, I felt the weariness of Brueghel's hunters. Cresting the hill that overlooked our frozen outpost, I saw their village. And, within its fortified boundaries, I watched men go about their daily tasks as if unaware of any higher purpose.

As THE TIME for Levi's trip home approached, the howitzer lieutenant correctly predicted that, rather than work anything out, we'd simply take another of his men to cover Levi's absence. He raised the impending issue with his headquarters. He did so via an email to the command sergeant major, requesting an increase in manpower to cover our requirement for a liaison. The lieutenant forwarded us the sergeant major's response, in which the sergeant major said that the only fucking way he'd even consider this horseshit request was if we provided him with written justification ASAP.

The chances of our providing justification, written or otherwise, to anyone, for anything, were zero. So the night before Levi went home, Hal and I paid another visit to the howitzer camp. That night, a blizzard clobbered Logar. I met Hal by the dog cages, as usual. The heavy snowfall had caused us to cancel that night's mission, and the dogs, who on off nights normally hurled themselves at the chain link, setting off the entire dog population of Logar, were still. Likewise, Hal was not himself. He shivered, and his scar was barely visible. When we reached the door of the howitzer camp, he had to knock twice.

The lieutenant answered. "Hey, guys. I'm really sorry about all this," he said.

"Yeah, yeah," Hal said. He poked his head in and saw a fat kid playing mah-jongg on a computer. "We'll take him."

"Uh, okay," the lieutenant said. "But the sergeant major's going to be pissed."

"Not my problem," Hal said.

Hal returned to the compound to sleep, and I waited outside until the kid pushed through the door with a variety of coffee mugs carabinered to the webbing of his ruck. "Ready!" he announced. And, with his headlamp on its brightest setting, we set off down the steep, icy road.

Falling snow converged to a vanishing point in the beam of the kid's headlamp. When he fell behind, I could almost reach out and touch this point. But then he'd trot up alongside me, mugs clattering, and it would recede. On one such occasion, he presented me with a handful of bullets.

"Can I trade these in for hollow-point?" he asked. "I

heard you guys roll with hollow-point. I also heard you guys muj up, in turbans and man jammies and shit, with MP5s tucked up in there. Like, *ka-chow*! That must be *wicked*!"

The kid fell behind, caught his breath, and trotted up beside me again.

"Can I get an MP5?" he asked.

I ushered the kid to the TOC and showed him Levi's computer. After booting up mah-jongg, he was quiet.

My next task was to put Levi on the rotator at dawn. The rotator was a cargo helicopter that ran a clockwise route around the AOR every morning. From our outpost, it would fly to Bagram, where Levi could catch a transport home. With daybreak less than an hour away, I poured myself a cup of coffee and sat back to watch the drone feed.

The drone was on the wrong side of the storm that sat over Logar, and its camera, which normally looked down on our targets, was searching a dark wall of cumulonimbus for a hole. Not finding one, it punched into the thick of the storm. For a moment, it seemed like it would be okay; then ice piled onto its wings as if a bricklayer had thrown it on with a trowel, and the drone hurtled toward earth. I wrote down its grid, because if it crashed we'd have to go out and fetch its brain. But as the drone fell into warmer air, the ice peeled away, and when it leveled off, its camera remained facing aft. I watched the drone pull a thread of the storm into clear morning air. By the time I heard the rotator's approach, the storm had passed.

Outside, covering everything, was a pristine layer of snow, which dawn had turned pink. I started the pink HiLux. I honked the horn, and it made a pink noise. Levi emerged from his pink tent with his pink ruck. I drove him down a pink road to the pink LZ. The rotator came in sideways, and its thumping rotors kicked up a thick pink cloud. Crouching, Levi and I ran through the cloud to a spot alongside the warm machine. A crewman opened the side door and handed me the mail, which included a package from Levi's mother. Then Levi hopped aboard and was on his way home.

The sun rose as I drove back to the TOC, and the whole outpost sparkled at the edge of the war. The stamps on the package from Levi's mother featured *Landscape with the Fall of Icarus*. The detail chosen was Icarus drowning. His legs kicked above the surface. The water looked cold and dark. What was not shown in the stamp was how the world went on without him.

The new liaison was asleep in Levi's chair when I got back. I opened the package quietly, so as not to wake him. More Kattekoppen. I put it on the shelf with the rest and was about to go to bed when the phones started ringing.

Two soldiers on their way home from a bazaar south of Kabul had taken a wrong turn. They'd hit a dead end and been ambushed. Bloody drag marks led from the scene, which was littered with M9 and AK brass. Witnesses said that the soldiers had been taken alive, which meant a rescue operation, led by us. We received pictures of the soldiers from a search-and-rescue database. One soldier had a chin and the other did not. The TOC filled with CIA, FBI, and ODA. Then a massive helicopter slung in the missing soldiers' ruined truck. Its windows had been shot through, and bullet holes riddled the skin. We opened the doors to find the smell of the missing soldiers still inside, along with the stuff they'd bought at the bazaar, intact in a flimsy blue bag.

The drag marks at the scene led to a tree line. The tree line opened onto a number of compounds, which we raided that night. Those compounds led to other compounds, which we raided the next day. The second set of compounds led to a village, which, overnight, we cleared. That delivered us to a mountain. It took two nights and a day to clear all the caves up one side and down the other. Which led us to another village. And so on.

Time became lines on a map leading in all directions from Chin and No Chin's ambush. Space existed only between those lines. We searched for the missing men night and day.

One night, west of Sangar, as we trudged through snow with the wind in our faces, an air-raid siren blasted, and a small village appeared in an explosion of light. The village, just beyond a tree line, seemed so peaceful as to mock me. Like, what are you afraid of, this stone wall? That donkey cart? Or was it the siren whose noise filled my lungs and poured out my open mouth? I radioed the howitzers for a fire mission.

"Send it," they replied.

I had coordinates for the village, and had I obeyed my instincts I would've transmitted them and brought heavy shells whistling down, but the leaves in the trees before me shone like silver dollars in the wind. And kids, awakened by the ruckus, quit their beds to run out under the streetlights. Women chased after those kids, leaving barefoot tracks in the snow. Had the women worn shoes I might've thought that the whole thing—village/light/siren—was a trick designed to set us up for an ambush, and I might've said "They're wearing shoes" over the radio, so that future patrols might know what to look for. But the women ran smiling and barefoot after their giggling kids. And men, appearing on their roofs, opened their arms to one another and shouted over the siren's blare: *Isn't this something!*

This, we later learned, was the unexpected restoration of power after months without—the opposite of a rolling black-out. The resulting commotion continued until one light went out, then another. Until the women had chased the kids inside and the men had waved goodbye. Until all the lights were out. Then someone shut down the air-raid siren, and its blare died to a whistle, and the whistle died to a tumble of bearings. After which all was dark and quiet.

"Send your fire mission," the howitzers repeated.

"Never mind," I said.

IF WE'D BEEN asked how long we'd go on searching, our answer would have been: as long as it takes. Think of the families back home. Baby Chin. Mother No Chin. But in truth there were limits, and we had methods for determining them. From the streaks of blood found in the drag marks, we ascertained wounds. From the wounds, we developed time-lines. And we presented these timelines on a chart, which read from top to bottom, best case to worst. By the time that village lit up beside us, we were at the bottom of the chart. The next night, we started looking for graves.

There was no time to sleep. My fingernails stopped grow-ing. My beard turned white. Cold felt hot, and hot felt cold. And, soon enough, I began to hallucinate. One night, as we approached a well, I watched Chin jump out and run away, laughing. Another night, I saw No Chin ride bare-ass up a moonbeam.

Meanwhile, the Mah-Jongg Kid had proved himself wor-thy by having the howitzers fully prepped for that pop-up non-ambush, and for every close call since. At first, I pre-ferred Levi's circles to M.J.'s hyperbolas, which opened onto an infinity that no howitzer could possibly reach. But then, as the search for our missing comrades wore on, producing only dry holes and dead ends, the idea of thrusting death some-where beyond the finite gained a sort of appeal.

We were down to almost nothing on the unwanted-food shelf. Only Kattekoppen and some kind of macaroni that re-quired assembly were left by the time we found No Chin's body in a ditch outside Maidan Shar.

No Chin had a note in his pocket indicating the where-abouts of Chin. We would find Chin, it said, buried under a tree by a wall. We hiked to trees without walls, walls without trees, graveless walls, and treeless graves, until finally, by a process of elimination, we stumbled on the right combination and dug.

Under a thin layer of dirt was a wooden box. Crammed inside the box was Chin. His last name was embroidered on his uniform, for all to read. But no one read it aloud. Because to do so, it seemed, would've reduced the whole thing to a name. As if we wouldn't have given our lives for a man whom none of us had known. One we hadn't expected to find alive, yet we'd all hoped to find alive. And we were sorry to see him go.

Prior to the mission, I'd filled my pockets with Kattekop-pen, which came in handy, because Chin had been dead for a while. Long enough to leave him covered with malodorous slime. The smell only got worse as our medics lifted Chin out of the box and slid him into a bag. Lex, Tull, and Hugs gagged. Hal, of all people, let loose a slender arc of bile. But I popped a steady supply of Kattekoppen, which kept the stink at bay.

THE NEXT MORNING, when the rotator arrived, we slid Chin in one door and Levi hopped out the other.

The snow had melted and the sun shone down on a muddy

world. It promised to be a bright, warm day. Levi and I got into the HiLux, and on the ride away from the LZ, I congratulated him and asked how it felt to be a father.

"It is strange," Levi said. "I have never much worried, but sefferal times a night now I wake up afraid the boy is dead. And I sneak into his room and, like this"—he wet an index finger and held it under his nose—"I check his breeding."

"And he's okay?" I said.

Levi sat hunched over, with his knees above the dash. "Yes," he said.

I looked out the windshield at the war, which, stamp-wise, could've been a scene from Brueghel's *Triumph of Death*—one that, without a skeleton playing the hurdy-gurdy, or a wagon full of skulls, or a dark iron bell, still raised the question of salvation. At the smoldering trash pit, I turned right, onto the road that ended at the artillery range.

"We will make a fire mission?" Levi asked.

"Correct," I said.

Excited, Levi got out the big green radio and started messing with freqs. I parked at the edge of the range, where the ashen hulks of what might once have been tanks had been bulldozed into a pile. Presumably, the same dozer that had cleared these wrecks had also scraped the giant concentric rings in the field of mud before us. Way out on top of the bull's-eye was our target, Chin and No Chin's truck, right where I'd asked for it to be slung.

Hal and I had met at the dog cages the night before to

discuss the rise of M.J., and whether or not Levi still had a place with us. While the dogs had rolled around, we'd devised this test.

I sat on the hood of the HiLux as Levi shot a bearing to the target with his compass and gauged the winds by the smoke blowing off the trash pit. Then he called it in, his Dutch accent somehow thicker after two weeks in Texas. But the howitzers' read-back was good. And, soon enough, iron scratches appeared against the clear blue sky. I followed them to impact, where fountains of mud ascended out of white-hot flashes. The mud fell, the booms rolled by, and I saw that the hits were good: the truck was badly damaged.

Still, enough of it remained to be hit again, without question. While Levi questioned, the magnetic pole upon which his bearing was anchored drifted ever so slightly; the breeze against which he'd applied his correction stiffened, and the men cradling the heavy shells of his next barrage cursed the unknown reasons for the holdup.

Rib Night

———

Sharana, Afghanistan

A fight broke out on the far side of the dining facility, over by the milk. A fridge door slapped shut, followed by sounds of shoving and punches being thrown. Soldiers dodged out of the way before a few brave souls went in to break it up. There were noises of slipped holds and flail, of tables and chairs scraping across the concrete floor. Then Digger's voice rang out—*I'll kill you!*—and for a moment it seemed like this night, a Friday, was about to transcend all its false promises.

Every Friday was rib night at this DFAC. Soldiers spent all day making the sauce, marinating the ribs, and stoking mesquite embers in split oil drums. They baked a cake the size of a garage door. They decorated the DFAC—a giant white tent—with balloons and streamers. They went to all this trouble, I knew, with good intentions. They wanted us to feel appreciated, and to give us a taste of home. They wanted us to enjoy, at least, the illusion of a party—as if this were a real Friday night, with an actual weekend to follow, and we might find it within ourselves to break a few weekday rules. Fighting, however, was prohibited.

Tables and chairs were being moved back to where they belonged, and a new line was forming for the milk. Digger walked over to where Hal and I sat, where we always sat, by the Jell-O cart.

"No one waits their goddamn turn anymore," Digger said. The collar of his T-shirt appeared to have been balled up and jerked around. Bright red scratches swelled on his neck. His eyes were red and bleary, like he hadn't slept.

"You all right?" Hal asked.

"I'm fine," Digger said.

Digger set a partially crushed carton of chocolate milk on the table. He laid down his cardboard tray, scattered with a few ribs he must've salvaged off the floor. He sat across from me, and flies settled on his ribs.

"I can't eat this," Digger said.

I'd tripled up on trays to prevent rib grease from soaking through. I separated the bottom tray and loaded it with half my ribs. Hal gave half his ribs, too. Digger—on the backside of the adrenaline rush that had fueled his fistfight—was staring off into nowhere, so I reached across the table and slid his old tray aside. Flies lifted off those ribs and spun their little orbits. Digger tilted a bit in his seat. As I pushed the new tray in front of him, his mouth dropped open and his eyes closed.

The DFAC was packed with soldiers who'd spent all day in the summer sun. Their faces were shiny with sweat, their eyes wild with heat exhaustion. Their laughter bounced off the tent's taut skin, reverberated in its aluminum frame, and rattled the turnbuckles, S-hooks, and galvanized wire that held the whole thing together. Hal dropped one clean bone after another at the center of the table. Flies walked across Digger's face to drink from the corners of his mouth. He'd been up all night the night before, on that mission out in Wardak, then up all day wrestling demons in the heat. Tired as he was, he'd fought that poor guy over by the milk.

Digger appeared to skip the early stages of sleep—in which his body would've cooled, his heart rate slowed—to plunge directly into REM. His eyes shifted as he began to dream. I watched them draw triangles under their lids.

Around two a.m. that morning, during a raid on a compound out in Wardak, Digger had killed three men in a room. They were sleeping in three corners, with an AK-47 resting on the floor in the center of the room, when Digger crept in. The first man in the first corner woke, reached for the AK, and Digger shot him. The next man in the next corner reached, and Digger shot him, too. The third man's fingers were almost touching the weapon when he died.

I heard the shots from where I stood, outside the walls of that compound, with Hal. Each shot sounded like when you walk into a dark room, flip a switch, and the filament in the bulb pops. I went into the room after the fact. Seeing the men reaching out for that AK, in death, I figured there had to have been some sort of conversation between them. Like, who would sleep in what corner, and where would they put their only weapon, the muzzle of which had been wrapped in orange wire, in what seemed to me a superstitious way. Like the wire had transformed the AK into a good luck charm, and the men had seen fit to leave it at the center of the room, beyond arm's length of any one of them, so that the good luck might extend to them equally. Yet they'd all reached for the AK when Digger had snuck into the room.

We searched the compound and found nothing. We took digital fingerprints of the dead men and beamed them back to Higher, who ran them through the database. Results were inconclusive. From the compound, we walked a mile through tall grass to where the helicopters would pick us up. An owl circled overhead in twilight, until the helicopters dropped out of the sky and scared it away. Digger and I climbed into the same helo and sat across from one another in the cargo bay. Sunrise through the window behind me lit Digger's stoic face as we flew back to Sharana.

It was already hot by the time we'd arrived at our outpost on the north end of the runway, where we lived in old shipping containers. Mine smelled as if it had been used to transport pepper. I stood my rifle in a corner and propped my armor against a wall. I closed the shipping container's heavy metal door and lay down on my cot. I fell into as deep a sleep as the heat of the day would allow. My dream was short-circuiting.

It went like this: We walked uphill into a village at night. A woman ran downhill, into our ranks, and searched the troop for me. I was the one wearing all the antennas. I was the one who'd talked to the plane that had shot up her house. I could see smoke rising from her house on the hill. Inside, in the corner of a room, a dead grandfather held his dead grandson. It was the daughter/mother who'd found me. It was she who'd insisted that I come inside her house to see what I'd done.

I'd brought an A-10 down for a thirty-millimeter strafe on four enemy standing at the top of the hill. The attack had killed three and left the fourth severely wounded. The wounded man was trying to drag himself to cover. He was bleeding from an artery in his shattered leg. I could've done nothing, and he would've died soon enough. Instead, I'd brought the A-10 back for another strafe. Rounds had drifted into the house. They'd found the boy and his grandfather hiding in the corner. The woman had run out of the house to find me.

I didn't want to go into the house because I knew it wouldn't do anyone any good, and I was right. But the woman's grief was so profound, it resembled joy. I couldn't ignore her, and I didn't want to push her away. Nor did I want to threaten her, then be in a position where I might have to carry out those threats. So I followed her up the hill, through the disintegrated wall of her house, and into a clouded room. I walked over shattered tiles toward the corner, where she pointed. There, I discovered the grandfather and grandson alive.

The grandfather brushed dust off his grandson's shoulders. *Can I help you?* he asked, like stray thirty mike-mike blew through his house all the time. Then—*bzzt!*—the dream short-circuited, and we were walking uphill into the village again, and the woman was running downhill to meet us halfway.

Somewhere in there, Digger entered my shipping container, which woke me up. Light and heat streamed through the open door.

"What?" I asked.

"I need a pill," Digger said.

My duffel bag lay against the wall opposite my armor. From it, Digger removed my flannel shirt. He searched the pocket where I kept my sleeping pills.

"I don't have any more," I said.

"Bullshit," Digger said. "Hal says he gave you, like, twenty."

Digger dumped the contents of my duffel bag onto the floor. Car keys chimed against the plywood. My wallet flopped open. Live 5.56- and nine-millimeter rounds rolled out the door and into the sun.

SOME CALLED THE pills "time machines"; others called them "TKOs." They were tiny blue ovals coated in shine. Standard issue was ten pills per man, and no more, because they were addictive. But the pills helped us get over the jet lag resulting from our long trip to Afghanistan. They eased our transition to the nocturnal schedule on which the success of our mission relied. And they rendered us comatose, and dreamless, when, for whatever reason, we couldn't sleep.

Every time we deployed a medic would issue these pills, in little plastic bags, as we boarded the cargo jet that would deliver us from our home base in Virginia to the war. We always left home around midnight. This last time, my fourth, it was March. Frost hung in the air. Stars tangled in the bare branches of the tallest oaks. Hal received his pills from the medic and stuffed them in his backpack. Digger tucked his plastic bag of pills into the front pocket of his jeans. I buttoned mine into the pocket of my flannel shirt, and when I looked up, there was Digger, looking back at me. "Here we go again," he said, smiling. Together we climbed the stairs into the dimly lit cargo bay.

We took off, refueled high over the continental shelf, then drilled eastbound through the stratosphere. Halfway across the black Atlantic, as others slept on the cold metal floor of the cargo bay, I stood at the starboard jump door, looking out its little round window at the night.

Swells rose on the surface of the moonlit ocean. Silver clouds whispered by. I removed the plastic bag from my shirt pocket and shook out a sleeping pill. It appeared gray in the moonlight. I swallowed it, then stayed at the window, waiting for it to take effect.

Honeycombs, checkerboards, and cobwebs spun before my eyes. The moon set, the sun rose. Clouds vaporized and the sea turned red. I saw the City of Atlantis, the Colossus of Rhodes, and the Pyramids of Giza, covered in gold. I saw the Tower of Babel, its top spiraling toward the heavens. I knew these things were real because I could press my hand against the jump door and feel the cold sky pressing back.

I kept the remainder of the pills in the pocket of my flannel shirt, in my duffel bag, against the wall of my shipping container. Spring was mild in Sharana, so the transition to sleeping days was easier than it would've been during summer. Every morning when we returned to the outpost, however, after both good nights and bad, the restlessness was the same. I'd sit on my cot and consider taking a pill, even though I knew that I wouldn't be able to stop. Even though I understood that after I ran out of pills, I wouldn't be able to find any more. In the end, I decided not to take one. And I slept well knowing that I had some in reserve.

Then came that night, in April, out near Shkin, when I brought the A-10 down for a second strafe, and rounds drifted into that house. And the noise arrived after the rounds hit, like a fart in the bathtub. And the woman ran downhill into our ranks, her screams no different than laughter.

I saw her twisted face by starlight. I saw smoke rising from her house as an infrared blur on night vision. She reached out to me, which I shouldn't have allowed, because she could've triggered my rifle, or pulled the pin on one of my

grenades. Instead, she touched my arm, and her grief transferred wholesale. I sensed the absence of her father and son,
and I felt her wish that I could bring them back. Had I wished
hard enough she might've felt me wishing the same thing.
Still, it seemed possible. The A-10 was still in the sky. We
were still walking uphill. Although I knew better, I followed
the woman into her house.

Returning to my shipping container after sunrise that
morning, I didn't care about the ramifications, I intended to
take a pill. I opened my duffel bag, dug out my flannel shirt,
and discovered the pocket empty. Ditto for the other pocket
of that shirt, and all the pockets of my other shirts. I thought
that maybe, in a blind fit of self-preservation, I might've hidden the pills somewhere so perfect that even I couldn't find
them. Then I remembered Digger, in line to board the cargo
jet back in Virginia, turning around.

I walked over to Digger's shipping container and banged
on its big orange door. He answered in his underwear.
"Yeah?" he said.

"Did you take my pills?" I asked.

"Your what?"

Looking into Digger's eyes, I saw seahorse tails spinning
clockwise.

"You know what," I said.

Digger blinked, and those tails spun the other way.

"I get all I need from Hal," Digger said. He shut his door
and barred it from the inside.

I walked to Hal's shipping container, which stood out in the wind. Blowing sand struck the broad side of it, making a noise like a finger circling the rim of a wineglass. The heavy door gonged when I knocked. Hal cracked it open just far enough to peek out. I explained my situation.

"I gave all my pills to Digger," Hal said.

"I just need one," I said.

On missions, Hal wore the same antennas as me. The woman who ran downhill into our ranks could've just as easily chosen him as the focus of her grief. She could've reached out and touched his arm.

"Hold on," Hal said, and he shut the door.

Putting my ear to Hal's door, I heard what sounded like Hal putting his ear to the other side of the door, wondering how long I'd wait. Meanwhile, the sun froze in the sky. The wind stopped blowing. The door popped open, and Hal released a blue pill into my cupped palm.

Back in my shipping container, I sat on my cot with the pill in my hand. I envisioned the honeycombs and checkerboards. I imagined Alexander the Great, riding his elephant down from the mountains into battle. I considered what the next morning would be like, trying to fall asleep without a pill, and I wondered where I might find more. Tearing a piece of duct tape from a roll, I stuck the pill to the ceiling over my cot. The little blue capsule was perfectly hidden between the gray tape and the gray steel. As I drifted off to sleep, only I knew it was there.

The steel walls of my shipping container turned to glass in my dream. I found myself alone on the barren steppe where Sharana once stood. The sun rolled backward across the sky. Night fell, frost formed on the glass, and it began to snow. A glacier descended from the mountains to bury me in ice for an eon before the thaw delivered a millennium of flood and driving rain. Then, one day, the clouds broke and the sun shone down on a forest of petrified baobabs. That night, the harvest moon crashed into the earth, smashing it to smithereens. I drifted in my glass box through space and time toward a tiny, blue, oval-shaped star that shone in the distance.

And that was the pill that Digger wanted, on that hot morning in June, after he'd killed three men out in Wardak.

SOMEONE HAD GONE to great lengths to find helium; then to inflate each red, white, and blue balloon, tie their nozzles, and knot them to strings. The other ends of the strings were tied to stones the way you might tie a threatening note to a brick before throwing it through a window. The stones anchored the balloons to the tables. The balloons floated over piles of bones. More soldiers entered the DFAC, and the heat coming off their fevered bodies threatened to lift the whole tent off the ground like an airship. All that commotion, and somehow Hal licking his fingers clean was what jolted Digger awake.

"Need anything?" Hal offered, standing.

Digger shook his head. Once Hal was out of earshot, I asked him, "Did you find a pill this morning?"

"No," he said.

"Who'd you ask?"

"Everyone."

Earlier, Hal, Digger, and I had walked from our outpost to the DFAC, whose opaque skin glowed amber in the night. Along the way, we'd passed two privates kissing in the moon shadow of a T-wall. We'd passed three colonels smoking cigars, and a gaggle of majors playing horseshoes. Sergeants, silhouetted by flame, had grilled the ribs on split oil drums. Clouds of bittersweet smoke had flavored the night air.

Before entering the DFAC, we'd each cleared our pistols into a barrel full of sand. We'd dropped our magazines, pulled back our slides, and caught the rounds that flipped out of the chambers. Hal and I had pushed our rounds back in our magazines, but Digger had thrown his out over the HESCO barrier and into tent city where all the daywalkers slept.

Inside the DFAC, at the steam table, Digger had just pointed at what he wanted. No please or thank you to the privates in their hairnets and aprons, holding their tongs and serving forks. No wishing them happy hunting, as was customary. From the steam table, Digger had set off for the milk.

A row of industrial-size refrigerators, each packed with hundreds of those grade-school boxes of milk, stood adjacent to the steam table. Muddled lines of soldiers formed in front of each. Digger, I guessed, had picked his box of chocolate milk out from a distance. Maybe it had looked colder than the rest, or fresher. Maybe Digger had thought that, as a killer, he was entitled to whichever box he wanted. After all, he hadn't spent his day making barbecue sauce, or stoking fires, or baking a fucking cake. He hadn't blown up balloons or hung streamers. Someone must've cut in front of Digger and taken his box of milk.

Digger had probably drilled the guy in the jaw. That was his signature move, anyway, the jaw-drill. I'd seen him do it under a streetlight in Virginia Beach, at a gas station in Salt Lake City, and on a bridge in Milwaukee. When Digger put his back into it, it was devastating. So whoever had taken Digger's milk had probably hit the fridge door unconscious. And his tray of ribs had probably gone flying. Then came the brave souls to break up the fight. At that point, it must've looked to Digger like the entire population of the DFAC was closing in, which might've made it seem like it was him against the world. When he'd shouted, *I'll kill you,* I figured that he'd meant everybody.

Hal returned to our table with an extra tray of ribs for Digger and me to share. I took all the burned ones, and Digger took all the rare. The three of us ate, and made a big mess of bones on the table.

A gray-haired master sergeant carrying a walkie-talkie appeared. He was followed by a skinny PFC with a widow's peak and sleeves too long for his arms. The master sergeant pointed at Digger with the antenna of his walkie-talkie.

"This the guy?" he asked the PFC.

"Yeah," the PFC said.

"You need to come with me," the master sergeant said to Digger.

"I don't need to do shit," Digger said.

"That's how you want to handle this?" the master sergeant asked.

"Yup," Digger said.

The master sergeant radioed for security. The name GRIMES was embroidered on his camouflaged blouse. The PFC looked at us like he didn't know who we were, or where we came from, but he wanted in.

"This guy's mine," Hal said to Grimes, while pointing at Digger. "How about you and me figure this out at our level."

"How about you eat, and let me handle this," Grimes said.

"I'm just trying to save us both some ass pain," Hal said. "Incident reports, and all that bullshit."

"Assault is not bullshit," Grimes said.

This made Digger laugh, which made Hal laugh, too.

"You're not helping," Hal said.

Double doors swung open behind the steam table. Two soldiers backed into the tent, each supporting one corner of the gigantic cake that had been decorated to look like the

American flag. Knowing the routine, birthday girls and boys stood up from their tables and made their way toward the stage.

"Go tell them to wait," Grimes said to the PFC with the long sleeves, who walked off while shaking his head. Grimes turned to Digger. "You think you can just come in here and tune up one of my soldiers?"

"He started it," Digger said.

"That's not what I'm hearing," Grimes said. He held his walkie-talkie up to his ear and fiddled with the volume.

"Whatever's gonna happen, can you make it quick?" Digger said. "I got shit to do."

"Oh, it'll be quick, all right," Grimes said.

"How long you been doing this?" Hal asked.

At that, Grimes smiled. He almost laughed. Because to rise to the rank of master sergeant meant that Grimes had been in at least fifteen years, so he had to know that nothing ever happened quick. Army, navy, it didn't matter which service. Try as you might, there was always that unbeatable thing pushing back. Grimes had to know. So when I saw him smile, I thought he was going to sit down with us, and he and Hal were going to work things out. Then we'd all shake our heads over how fucked up everything was, and how we'd almost gotten caught up in it there, for a second.

A lieutenant with his own walkie-talkie appeared. He asked Grimes, "Are you ready for the cake, Master Sergeant?"

The cake, by then, was up on stage. Soldiers were sticking candles into it. A few dozen birthday girls and boys, all way too young, stood around, waiting for those candles to be lit and for the lights to go out and for all of us to sing "Happy Birthday," which happened on every rib night.

"Does it look like I'm ready for the goddamn cake?" Grimes said.

"I'm just asking," the lieutenant said.

"If I was ready for the fucking cake, do you think I'd be down here and not up there?"

"Sorry, Master Sergeant," the lieutenant said. "I didn't know."

The DFAC's aluminum frame creaked gently against the wind, as if it were being held down by ropes. As if, absent those ropes, we'd float away to a new and faraway place, where we might live by our own rules.

"Your attention, please!" the lieutenant yelled from the stage. No one paid attention. Then Grimes whistled, and everybody shut up.

"We're going to postpone the birthday celebration for a few minutes," the lieutenant announced, "due to a problem that we need to take care of first."

"That's me!" Digger shouted, climbing on top of our table. "I'm the problem!"

Soldiers booed and cheered. Digger held his arms open to them while turning a slow circle. Soldiers beat their tables with their fists.

"Fuck you if you're here to eat cake, and not to fight!" Digger yelled.

There were more cheers than boos this time, as Digger climbed down from the table and returned to his seat.

"See, now, that's where you and I agree," Grimes said to Digger. "You think they had birthday cakes in Nam?"

"Exactly," Digger said.

Grimes's walkie-talkie squawked. He put the speaker to his ear while looking at the DFAC's entrance, on the far side of the steam table. Finding no security there, Grimes turned to check the fire exit next to the stage. "I'm in the middle, by the Jell-O cart," Grimes said into the mike. "Where are you?"

They could've been on the ground, surrounded by cut ropes, watching us float away. They could've been asking themselves where the hell we thought we were going.

I couldn't speak for anybody else in the DFAC on rib night. But Digger, it was safe to say, had joined to fight. Hal had joined because if he hadn't, the war would've never been the same. And as for me, I'd joined to see the world.

Baker's Strong Point

—

Dugway Proving Ground, Utah

I'd said some things about Reed's true love the night before. So at breakfast, in the motel lobby, we didn't talk. We didn't talk loading the laser equipment into the government truck, either, or pulling out of the parking lot. I suppose if I'd been unsure of the way, Reed would've gotten out the map and told me where to go. But the signs through Wendover to I-80 eastbound were easy enough to follow. I cranked up my window in the merge, dropped the truck into fourth. The rising sun turned the windshield gold. I had to take it on faith that the highway unfolded in a long straight line before us.

This was our first trip to Baker's Strong, a bombing range in the southwest corner of the proving grounds. Dugway OPS had issued us the truck, along with a binder on all the ranges. Reed opened the binder for directions. He looked out the window. Phone poles shushed past, interspersed with gleaming piles of salt. The word INFIDEL was embroidered into the

back of his ball cap. Everything in the rearview mirror collapsed on a dot.

Reed broke the silence. "Take this dirt road," he said.

"Where?" I asked.

"Right here," he said, pointing.

A dirt road appeared. The sun rolled onto my left shoulder in the turn. We bumped off the easement and climbed up
a hill. We descended into a prehistoric lake that had evapo-
rated over millennia. Rings etched in the surrounding high
ground marked the waterline's gradual descent. All that remained was a wide bed of salt.

"Nineteen point seven miles to the OP," Reed said.

I reset the odometer. Reed closed the binder and pushed in
the lighter.

The OP, or observation point, overlooked the southern
end of the salt bed, on which a number of targets would be
arranged. Standing the laser at the OP, we'd shine it on one of
those targets. The laser beam would refract off whatever out-
of-service vehicle the target happened to be: half-track, earth-
mover, tank. Bombs from a B-52, scheduled to be overhead in
an hour, would then guide on the refracted energy. Fuses
would trigger warheads. Fireballs would bloom like mari-
golds, turning inside out and black.

The lighter popped.

"Listen, man," I said. "I'm sorry."

"For what?" Reed spoke out of the side of his mouth that

was not concerned with touching the cigarette to the lighter's red-hot coil.

"For what I said about Cheyenne last night."

I'd known Reed for five years by then. In that time, we'd made three deployments to Afghanistan together. While deployed, we'd controlled air strikes in support of night raids. We'd had good nights and bad. Mostly good, early on; then the bad nights had started to accumulate. Toward the end of our second deployment, they'd pulled about even. Midway through our third, bad nights had surpassed good. I didn't know how future deployments were going to play out, but the trend was worrisome. I couldn't help but extrapolate that trend five or ten years into the future, when Reed and I would be civilians who, on certain nights, would recall things that had happened during the war. Looking back on those things, I'd probably see good stuff as bad, and bad stuff as worse. Some nights I'd probably want to call Reed and talk about it. Or, maybe, talk about other things as a way of getting around to it. For example, that morning we drove to Baker's Strong OP—how the dust rose to a certain level in our wake. How the odometer, on every rotation, stuck at eight-tenths of a mile.

Reed filled his lungs with smoke, and held it. His eyes watered. He exhaled a stream, tight as wire, out the cracked-open window. "I'll admit," he said, "it's not an ideal situation."

"So how'd you leave it with her?" I asked.

"She's in my room with the gun."

———

HALF OF WENDOVER was in Utah, half in Nevada. A bright line painted across Main Street separated the two. The Nevada side had neon casinos, glittering strip clubs, fluorescent knife shows, et cetera. The Utah side had darker versions of the same things.

The Pump House was a cinder-block establishment on the Utah side, between the interstate and the railroad tracks. It was named for what it used to be. The pumps were long gone. Cut boards covered holes in the floor where pipes had risen from the ground. The music, I supposed, was at least as loud as the pumps would've been. A woman danced on a plywood stage in chrome heels. Others floated around in velvet capes, their faces turned purple by the black light.

I'd seen these women before, in Afghanistan, in the aftermath of an aerial bombardment. As I'd walked from my covered position toward the hissing point of impact—through bitter walls of smoke and over glowing rings of frag—these women had flown toward me. I didn't know where they'd come from, but I liked to think that in guiding the bomb to earth I'd released them from captivity. Maybe they'd slipped through the hole the bomb had torn between our world and another, or perhaps they'd waited—burrowed into the dirt like spores—for the bombs to fall. In any case, they had wings and they could fly. I watched them climb, dive, and roll over half-dead men, half-buried in the smoldering earth. I watched them weave through stands of burning trees. As they returned to me, their wings smelled like burnt hair. Their kisses felt cold. In war, I was their savior. At the Pump House, however, I was just another man whose questionable urges lay barely submerged.

Reed sat with me at the bar for a while, drinking beers, until Cheyenne walked by. He shouted at her over the music, "Don't I know you from somewhere?!"

Cheyenne's eyes shone silver in the black light. Her lips were shiny and full.

"I don't think so!" she shouted back.

REED CARRIED THE GPS in hand, and the laser designator in a backpack over his shoulder. I carried the laser spot tracker and the radio. The sun shone in our faces. We crossed sandy knolls dotted with scrub brush, following the GPS to the OP's coordinates.

"This is it," Reed said. He dropped his pack onto a sandy knoll among a thousand sandy knolls.

Trash left behind by previous controllers—spent D-cells, empty Rip It cans, rusty 40mm brass—surrounded the OP. We looked down on the salt basin, where, a half mile northeast, there ran a diagonal line of bombed-out targets. Misses on either side of the target line had cratered and scorched the salt. Chocolate mountains stood beyond the targets, on the far rim of the basin. The flawless blue sky narrowed their shadows into points.

Reed set up the designator, and I set up the tracker. The

tracker had a powerful zoom. Through it, I could see the targets clearly. Although the cannons were missing—along with the turrets, tracks, armor plates, and engines—the burnt frames were unmistakably tanks.

The designator had a scope, boresighted to the laser. Lying prone in the sand, ball cap backward, Reed aimed through the scope. He put the crosshairs on the target, then pulled the trigger. The laser clicked loudly. It operated outside the visible spectrum; therefore, it was hidden to the naked eye. Looking through the tracker, though, I could see it.

First, Reed aimed for a half-buried sprocket at the end of a cracked axle under the northernmost tank, but a rise in the middle distance caused the laser to skip. Next, he tried to paint a stanchion that connected the main chassis to the turret ring on the center tank, but the energy reflected straight down. After several more attempts to achieve a good refraction, he shut off the laser.

"These targets are shit," he said.

Twenty minutes remained until the B-52 was scheduled to drop. I powered down the tracker. "I'll go," I said.

Grabbing the radio, Reed said, "I'll come with."

THE MUSIC CONTAINED noises of a failing pump—the screech of cavitation, the whack of a thrown bearing, the rattle of a loose intake grate. A woman rolled on the stage, banging her heels against the plywood surface. Women waiting their turns to perform did so behind a curtain, in what must've once been the control room. The bartender chewed her nails behind the cash register. Over in the corner, on a sofa they had all to themselves, Cheyenne and Reed wiggled under the cover of her thick black cape.

A tattooed runt in a Raiders jersey entered. Ignoring the girl onstage, he stared at Reed and Cheyenne, whose head was thrown back, whose long brown hair hung loose upon her cape. Reed's boots stuck out from under the hem. The runt stood in the center of the room. He turned to the bartender, and she stopped chewing her nails. The runt pointed at the sofa.

"Does Bas know about this?" he asked.

REED CARRIED THE radio. I carried the tarp, the cord, and my knife. The radio was tuned to the frequency on which the B-52 would contact us. Static poured out of its speaker like sugar.

The salt basin was not what I'd expected. It was not the flat, milky surface it appeared to be from a distance. Rather, it reflected the sky. And it was made up of a billion salt teardrops stood on their pointy ends. These teardrops disintegrated into crystals under my boots.

A salt bridge between two craters led to the tank on which Reed and I would hang the tarp. We climbed inside its ashen frame.

Once upon a time, there'd been no such thing as a tank. Men had fought to a standstill using rifles, mortars, and artillery. Then someone had an idea to break through the lines: a heavily armored vehicle mounted with a cannon. So the first tank came to be, and it did its job well, until it was outgunned and outmaneuvered by a better tank. Then a new idea was hatched, and a new and improved tank came along. Eventually, that new and improved tank also became outgunned and outmaneuvered, requiring an even better tank, and so on. Some of the obsolete tanks wound up being sold to foreign nations—Egypt, Kuwait, Peru. Others decorated the lawns outside VFWs. Still others were sent here, to Baker's Strong, where they were crushed, burned, twisted, and melted back into ideas.

I unfolded the tarp, silver on one side and brown on the other, with eyeholes in the corners. I measured a length of cord. I pulled out the ivory-handled hunting knife that I'd taken off a dead Taliban one night on our last deployment, and I cut the cord. I tied a corner of the tarp, silver side facing the OP, to what remained of the turret ring.

"Can I see that?" Reed asked, holding his own length of cord.

Reed had taken an AK off a different dead man that same night. I folded my knife and passed it to him.

THE BARTENDER SHRUGGED in response to the runt's question regarding whether or not Bas knew about what was happening on the sofa. The runt then turned and left the Pump

House in a hurry. I shouted to Reed from my barstool. He popped his head out from under Cheyenne's cape.

"What?" he yelled over the music.

"Time to go!" I yelled back.

Noise smeared the space between us.

"What for?" Reed said.

"Her boyfriend's coming!" I said.

"What boyfriend?" Cheyenne hollered.

Cheyenne swore that she and Bas weren't a thing, and never had been. He was just a fat, dumb asshole from whom none of us had anything to fear. Still, she decided to leave work early. The bartender gave her a baseball bat from behind the register. Cheyenne handed the bat over to Reed. Reed insisted that we walk Cheyenne home.

We waited outside, by a power station, while Cheyenne changed out of her cape. High-tension wires bent down to connect with voltage converters. The buzzing converters tossed a carcinogenic heat.

"What happens when Bas shows up?" I asked Reed.

"We tune him up," he said.

"What about the five dudes he brings with?"

"There's no five dudes."

Reed tossed the bat into the air and caught it by the business end. He passed the bat to me, handle first. Although it was the most nonconductive thing imaginable—a wooden bat with electrical tape wrapped around the handle—it acted like an antenna. Thus, I received an image of Bas, sitting alone at his beat-up desk, in his shithole office, behind East Wendover's only muffler shop. I suppose he could've been the mayor of that side of town, which would've explained his overall weariness, as men like the runt were always running through the night to bring him bad news.

The door to the Pump House opened, and music blasted out. Cheyenne had tied her hair back into a ponytail and changed into jeans. She smiled at Reed in a way I'd never been smiled at, which made me wonder what I was doing wrong.

FIRST THING I did, upon returning to the OP, was draw the attack geometry in the sand. I'd learned this trick from Reed, years ago. It was his habit back then; now it was mine, as I'd found it harder and harder to keep things straight. With all the back-and-forth, that is, between the war and home, and training for the war, sometimes I couldn't pinpoint the year, or the season. Sometimes I even forgot where I was, and I had to stop and think. For example: western Utah, 2009.

I made a point in the sand to represent the OP. I made a point for Wendover, where the B-52 would begin its target run, and a point for the target, both at relative distances and bearings from the OP. I drew a vector in the direction the B-52 would fly—east-southeast—from Wendover to the target. I drew an arrow from the OP to the target, in the direction the laser would shine. My finger in the warm sand felt like summer, when, in fact, it was fall.

The radio crackled: "Bulldog Zero One, Lava Seven Two, single Stratofortress, twenty miles northeast of Wendover, sixteen thousand feet."

I briefed the attack, cleared the B-52 down to two thousand feet, and asked the pilot to report his arrival over Wendover, which was the entry point for the range. Looking through the tracker, I made one last check of the target area. Heat shimmered off the salt bed, liquefying the tanks. Wind bent the heat.

I CARRIED THE bat down the hill from the Pump House, following Reed and Cheyenne under the train trestles, around the water tower, and onto her street. She lived in a mobile home with lattice tacked over the wheels. A mirror ball in the front yard reflected the moon and stars. Cheyenne's neighbor's bloodhounds barked at us from their cages. I waited under the water tower while Reed went inside to say good night.

From the east, three locomotives pulled in a freight train, which clattered, screeched, and sparked, as a burgundy Cadillac rolled in from the west with its lights out. The Cadillac parked in front of Cheyenne's house. Its long door opened and Bas emerged. He hiked up his pants in the street. Cheyenne was right: he was fat. He walked, pigeon-toed, around the front of the car. Behind me, the freight train continued to rumble. Blue sparks from the train's wheels flashed in the mirror ball in Cheyenne's front yard.

The bloodhounds shook their cages, their barking drowned out by the train. Bas lumbered over a crooked line of paver stones that led to the stairs, which he climbed one at a time to the porch. Bas held open the screen door to knock shyly on the main door. No lights came on inside.

Reed might've forgotten all about Bas. He might've even forgotten about me. Bas went to the window, cupped his hands around his eyes, and looked inside. The train's reflection ran in one side of his head and out the other. He moved down the porch to the next window. The train ended, and as it continued westward, the street fell silent. I heard Bas breathing hard as he descended from the porch. I heard each stair creak under his weight. I saw the railing, made of galvanized pipe, shake. Bas stopped on the paver stones, halfway to his Cadillac. From there, he looked across the street right at me, standing under the water tower in a moon shadow. But that wasn't why Bas didn't see me. He was thinking about Cheyenne, and wondering who she was with. He was conjuring, for himself, an image of Reed, which made me invisible. Bas turned around and walked back toward the house.

I tried to stay on the balls of my feet. I tried to shoot in from the side, on an angle. But the bloodhounds heard me coming and they gave me away. Bas turned to see the bat over my head, right at the point of weightlessness.

"WENDOVER, INBOUND," THE pilot reported.

I radioed back, "Descend to five hundred feet and continue inbound."

Reed triggered the designator—*click, click, click*. The tracker registered a ball of energy where we'd hung the tarp. I looked up in the sky where the B-52 should've been: three hundred thousand pounds of metal, trailing a curtain of soot.

"You see him?" Reed asked, aiming through the scope.

"Not yet," I said.

REED AND I sat on the Cadillac's hood, waiting for Cheyenne to pack her stuff. The bloodhounds mumbled in their cages. Bas lay unconscious in the dirt, on his back. In his waistband, I'd found an ivory-handled revolver, which I gave to Reed, whose face appeared among the moon and stars in the mirror ball.

"What's your plan?" I asked Reed.

"Take her back to the motel."

"Then what?"

"I don't know."

Reed rolled the revolver's cylinder under his thumb.

"How about you give her the car, and the gun, and let her go."

Reed thought about it. "I can't just let her go."

"Why not?" I asked.

"She needs my help."

I thought about the dark angels in Afghanistan: how, after being released from wherever they'd come, they'd fold in behind me. How they'd whisper things that made me feel like a savior.

"She doesn't need your help," I said. "She just needs another dumbass to believe her bullshit."

THE SKY OVER Baker's Strong was empty. No B-52, no moon, no clouds. Just blue, but not uniformly so. It was dark at the edges, like the void beyond was peeking through. Looking into that void, I imagined Cheyenne back in Reed's motel room. She was sitting on the corner of the bed with the pistol in her lap, staring at the locked door. Or maybe she was on the highway, with the windows down, and she had to keep brushing her hair out of her face to see where she was going.

Reed was still looking through the scope while firing the laser. "It's gotta be right fucking there," he said.

And there it was: as unnatural as a castle suspended in midair. With its walls, gatehouses, drawbridge, and moat, suspended. With the earthen mound on which it was built, suspended, its underside whiskered in shadowed roots. With all its red flags blowing in the wind.

Great Circle Route Westward Through Perpetual Night

Kandahar, Afghanistan

They piped all the shit into a reservoir. When the reservoir was full, they poured diesel on top of the shit and lit it on fire. The diesel burned, and the shit turned to vapor. The vapor rose and condensed into clouds. The clouds thickened, forming drops heavy enough to fall to earth. Then the stars disappeared and it rained shit. This happened often enough. This happened at night, whenever the shit reservoir was full.

Mir's memorial took place on such a night. Mir was a Belgian Malinois, trained by monks. The monks taught Mir to obey voice commands and hand signals. They taught him to sniff out bad intentions in men. The monks sold Mir to us for a king's ransom, and we took him to Afghanistan. There, Mir found booby traps, machine gun nests, and false walls. There, Mir flung himself at barricaded shooters. Nights the wild dogs howled, Mir did his best to ignore them, same as us. Then one night one of our own guys, Big Country, shot

Mir. The next night it rained shit and we held Mir's memorial.

The ceremony occurred in the plywood hut where we
briefed our missions. First to arrive, I turned on the lights.
The intelligence that had been used to brief the previous
night's mission still hung on the wall. Pictures of the men we
were after hung in a row. The satellite image of the compound in which we thought we'd find those men was stapled
next to their pictures. That image had been captured by the
satellite in summer. There were leaves on the trees in the compound's courtyard. Now it was autumn, almost winter, and
those trees were bare. A map of the Helmand River valley,
hanging next to the satellite image, showed the patrol route
we were supposed to have followed. That route began at a
point in the valley's eastern foothills—where the Chinooks
had dropped us off—and continued west in a long blue line
toward our target compound by the river.

Two Chinooks carried us forty miles north of Kandahar
and into the mountains. They dropped us off at midnight in a
high meadow, five clicks east of our target compound. We
filed westward across the dry grass. Passing through a narrow
saddle, we descended into the valley.

The stars were so bright we could've gone unaided. Still,
night vision afforded certain advantages. I saw ice crystals
trailing off the drone's wingtips, meteor showers in the iono-
sphere, plasma connecting unnamed constellations. Down in

the valley I observed wind, not just playing on the corn, but the actual movement of air in evergreen loops. The sky was jade, the faraway mountains aluminum, the river like something you'd see out the window of a time machine.

I was at the center of the single-file formation, following Big Country with his M60 slung over his chest, and belts of seven-six-two crossed on his back. Big Country followed Hal, who followed Goon, and so on up to Able and Mir. Frank walked behind me. Descending through the foothills, we passed caves that tunneled deep into the mountains, and wide-open shafts that dropped a hundred feet to underground canals. Wild dogs perched on ridgelines. Meanwhile, rocks gave way to stones, and stones to dirt. The dirt ended in a tall cornfield.

We didn't know what was hidden in the corn, so Able unleashed Mir, and Mir slipped into the crop at a sprint. He ran a search pattern—visible in the shaking tassels, audible in the torn leaves—of ever-widening scope. When we were no longer able to see or hear Mir running through the corn, Hal signaled: *Move.* We entered the cornfield on a tractor path that started out wide and flat but soon became narrow and rutted. Corn closed in on either side, bending to touch overhead. On a long thin curve, I lost sight of Big Country and Frank. I continued on course, or what I thought was on course. After it seemed like I'd walked a full circle, the path turned the other way; then the path became less of a path and more like the space between stalks.

I stopped walking, shut my eyes, and listened. I felt the separation between my troopmates and me increasing. The part of me that was always telling myself that I didn't belong, that I'd never belong, whispered those things to me. The wind died down, the corn fell still. Stars jumbled overhead. I considered breaking radio silence, disrupting the mission, exposing us to detection and possible attack. Then I heard something running at me through the corn.

I stared through the goggles in the direction of the noise. The corn was diseased. The thermal image of blight was an effervescent black. Whatever was running my way was not human. I felt its charge reverberate in the ground. It seemed too big to be Mir, but then again, I'd never been on this end of his attack. I took a knee in the mud and tried to remember Mir's safe word—*Lollipop? Oklahoma?* I raised my rifle to my cheek. A switch on the front grip activated both the infrared floodlight and the laser. A switch on the trigger grip released the safety. I stared through one night-vision tube, and through my holographic sight, into the corn. The laser dazzled at the center of the infrared beam, creating the impression of a portal between worlds, through which I might escape. Metal warmed against my cheek. I took the slack out of the trigger, gently. I tried not to think. Then Mir appeared: wild, shining, suspended like a quicksilver dog. Splashing off a mud puddle, he turned away.

I flipped the safety on and lowered my rifle. I stood, and

walked toward the river. Still lost, I found myself at the edge of an open field, where crows were propped like suitcases amid rows of stubble. Spotting one of my teammates on the opposite side of the field, I reached for an IR chem light to signal: *Friendly.* But he cracked his first. And there was Big Country, bathed in infrared waves, holding his chem light like a votive. The image of his face on my night vision alternated between a bronze and a tin mask. His shadow surged over the cornstalks behind him, while the shadows of crows surged my way.

A KNOCK SOUNDED on the plywood door of the hut where the memorial was soon to begin. I opened the door to find a new chaplain standing in the shit rain.

"May I come in?" he asked.

Once inside, the new chaplain wanted to know who I was, and where I was from. I could've asked him the same thing. The old chaplain—taller, happier—had shown up at the beginning of deployment to take down our names, points of contact, and next of kin. This information went into a sealed envelope that, the old chaplain had assured us, would be destroyed in the event of our safe return home. Then he'd asked us to bow our heads and pray for our safe returns, which, I remembered thinking, would've made me feel like a phony if I'd done it, and would've made me feel like an asshole if I hadn't. This new chaplain, though, didn't seem like the sort who'd force anybody to pray. In fact, the very idea of prayer seemed to have worn him down. I told him who I was, and where I was from.

"Never been there," he said.

"You should go sometime," I said. "There's a boardwalk with rides," I continued, leaving out all the fistfights that went on in the parking lots. "And the ocean's warm in summer." I failed to mention the trash that occasionally floated ashore. "And there's this beach where, on the night of a full moon, one wave will leave a million silver minnows flipping in the sand, and the next wave will carry them all back out to sea."

"Sounds great," the chaplain said, looking around the plywood hut. "Where do you want me to sit?"

I unfolded three chairs—one for the chaplain, one for Hal, and one for Able—and placed them against the front wall.

"And is there a lectern or some such?" the chaplain asked.

I dragged the podium out from behind a stack of busted swivel chairs in the corner, and I centered it at the front of the room. Taking his place behind the podium, the chaplain looked out at the rows of empty benches. He must've imagined the audience, who'd be looking to him for answers.

"So, tell me what happened," the chaplain said.

I CRACKED MY chem light and shook it. Big Country signaled: *Come*. I crossed the muddy field, stubble folding under my boots. Crows hopped aside. I felt relieved, even happy. That's when Mir flew out of the corn, on a white-hot line toward Big Country.

The 60's muzzle flash resembled an orchid bloom. Mir folded in half. Crows leapt into the air, flapping their huge black wings, as the boom echoed.

"I'M SORRY," THE chaplain said.

By now my teammates were entering the room, one by one and in pairs, to sit where they always sat—breachers with breachers; snipers behind them; Rangers, minus Big Country, in the back rows. Hal entered, carrying the ammo can that contained Mir's ashes. He set it on the podium. Able arrived with a plug of chewing tobacco in his lower lip, and a paper cup to spit in. I sat in the middle row. Chuck wandered in and sat next to me.

Chuck was a civilian contractor in his sixties. His last war had been Vietnam, where he'd done PSYOP, which, as far as I could gather from the stories he'd told, had entailed walking through villages naked and unarmed in broad daylight and spray-painting oxen gold. Afterward he'd gone off to a ranch in Texas, where he'd cleared brush, watered cattle, and driven the plow. Now he was our camp commandant, responsible for the day-to-day upkeep of our tiny compound within the larger FOB, and arguably the best one we'd ever had. Because Chuck knew the difference between those things we needed (hot water, clean shitters, 120 VAC) and those things we wanted (NFL cheerleaders, broadband, tins of bear meat) and those things we didn't even know we wanted.

Chuck leaned over. "Who wants an orange whip?" he whispered.

"Me," I said.

"We'll go right after this."

The ammo can containing Mir's ashes was decorated with photos. In one, Mir held the windpipe of a barricaded shooter between his jaws. Blood covered his muzzle, thick as paint. Dust caught in the flash on that dark night looked like stars. In another, Mir licked beans from Able's plate at a barbecue back home in Virginia. In a third photo, taken from Able's helmet-cam during an assault on a farmhouse outside Shkin, Mir lunged at some poor Taliban who'd just lifted himself from his hiding place in the muck. Who, if I remembered right, managed to sprint a few yards before a hail of bullets twisted him off his feet.

BIG COUNTRY AND I knelt in the mud on opposite sides of Mir. Big Country dug in his med pouch. I kept pressure on the exit wound with one hand while talking on the radio with the other. I tried to tell everyone where we were and what had happened, but my thumb kept slipping off the transmit button. I used the crows, circling overhead, to reference our position. But there were other crows circling other fields. Able crashed through the corn first. He shoved me out of the way.

"I'm sorry," Big Country said to Able. "I thought—"

"Get him out of here," Able said to me.

As I walked with Big Country across the field, the noises of the lifesaving effort fell away. Standing in a far corner, Big Country closed his eyes and sighed. I told him it was a mistake anyone could've made and Big Country took a deep breath. Then he started, very softly, to roll his lips in scales. Low to high, *do re mi . . .* , then high to low, as if warming up to sing. He scrunched his shoulders and let them drop. He stretched his face into smiles and frowns. He rolled his lips— *brrreee, brrrray, brrraaa.* It was all very soft and private, with his eyes still closed, which made me want to walk away. Later, Big Country's boys explained to me that his dream was to star on Broadway. That he did those exercises to keep his voice strong, so that he could audition when his army career was over. Had I walked away from Big Country, I would've never known.

IN HIS INVOCATION, the chaplain called God "the author of life." Hal told a joke, then opened it up to the rest of the troop. We sat on the wooden benches, looking up at the ammo can on the podium, waiting for someone to go first. That someone was Frank, with his boxer's nose and his big Hawaiian shirt.

Frank reminisced about the night Mir had torn open the barricaded shooter's throat. This had happened at a walled compound at the base of the Khost bowl, under a new moon.

The shooter had hidden behind a woodpile in the far corner of the courtyard. He opened up on us from there as we filed through the gate. Frank's recollection differed from mine in that Frank felt like he was walking on the moon, whereas I felt like I was at the bottom of the sea. Regardless, we agreed on one key point: what had driven Mir to launch himself at the triggerman, and kill him so viciously, had been love, pure and simple.

Next, Chuck told the story about a mutt who'd lived on the range in Texas, where Chuck had spent the decades between Vietnam and Afghanistan. Chuck explained how, leaving the mutt behind at the house, he'd ride off on horseback to mend distant fences. Not even Chuck knew when he'd be back. Yet this mutt, who apparently lay on the front porch from one unchanging day to the next, did. Furthermore, the mutt knew, from three hundred and sixty degrees of total emptiness, the direction from which Chuck would return. Walking this line, the mutt would meet Chuck halfway. Chuck ended his story there, leaving us to imagine their reunion on a dry, level plain, where shade cast by tall clouds crept over scattered rocks. After Chuck, it was my turn.

I told the story of how Mir had once bitten my hand. This had happened on a winter's night, at an outpost high in the mountains bordering Pakistan. I was outside, in the snow, walking to the shitters. Starlight had fallen on Able and Mir walking toward me. As we'd converged, Mir had wheeled around and chomped my hand. His teeth had hit bone, and it had stung like a motherfucker. I'd said as much, loudly. Able had stopped walking and turned on his headlamp.

"What?" he'd asked.

"Fucker bit my hand," I'd said.

Able had shone his light on Mir, bug-eyed and panting steam. Then he'd turned his light on my hand. Through the fog of my own breath, I was surprised to find the skin unbroken. I was surprised that my hand was not on fire.

During my eulogy for Mir, I talked about how sharply that bone had stung. How that sting had spread to every other bone in my hand. How it had risen into the bones of my arm and neck. How the pain had almost made me feel bad for the enemy.

Subsequent eulogies turned into calls for revenge. The inevitability of this saddened me more than Mir's death, or the fact that the men we'd been after the night before had escaped. In all likelihood, they'd spooked after hearing the 60's report. We'd found their warm bedrolls in a tearoom. Their phone booth odor had lingered, but without Mir we were unable to track it into the night. Now we'd have to hunt those men down and kill them, one by one. Then hunt down their fathers and sons. Then their cousins and uncles, and so on.

As the penultimate eulogy wound to an unforgiving close, Able tilted in his seat, looking a little slack-jawed. He was either lost in thought or half-asleep. Probably the latter, since he'd stayed awake all day. Not only had he lost his best friend, he'd carried his bagged-up remains to the morgue, and waited for Mir to be cremated. He'd walked his ashes back to the camp. Then, while he was on the phone to the States, arranging for Mir's replacement, he'd searched the hard drive for photos to decorate the ammo can. He'd printed those photos, cut them out, and taped them to the sides, all the while thinking about what he was going to say for the eulogy.

Hal elbowed Able and pointed to the podium: *Your turn.* Able looked at the podium as if he'd never seen such a thing. The plug of chewing tobacco, poking out from his lower lip, appeared cold and whiskered. Able used his tongue to roll it into his paper cup. Standing, he set the cup on the seat of his folding chair. He walked a bent line to the podium, and stared out at us through bloodshot eyes.

"It was a Tuesday, three years ago. November," Able began.

He'd left our compound in Virginia Beach at zero four and driven all the way into the Green Mountains of Vermont. The leaves were all sorts of colors. He'd reached the monastery gates around noon, and parked across the street. The wrought iron bars were topped with angels. There was a call box on the stone pillar to his right. He'd pushed the button and said, "I'm Dave Jones from Poseidon Security," or whatever the cover story was at the time. "I'm here for the dog."

The monk on the other end of the call box was like, "Great. We just need you to come inside and complete our assessment."

Able had picked up dogs from the monks before. He'd

done all of their assessments. He knew that the monks would sit him down in their little classroom and ask their little questions. *What are your shortcomings? How do they prevent you from being a better person? What does it mean to be a better person?* Able understood the rationale behind this line of questioning—that his limitations, via his interactions with the dog, would become the dog's limitations. That only through a constant process of self-improvement would he and the dog evolve into a truly effective team. Able did not necessarily agree with this philosophy, which the monks liked to call "the mirror." But he had to hand it to them. They'd built a highly successful operation upon it.

The monastery gates had parted, revealing a world unto itself. Able had stood at the threshold of that world in a blue work shirt. The patch over his left pocket had advertised: POSEIDON. The name tag over his right pocket had been embroidered: DAVE. Through falling maple leaves, Able had looked down the road that led to the ivy-covered bell tower. Previously, he'd walked down that road, around the bell tower, and into the classroom. Previously, he'd admitted to the following shortcoming: he couldn't let things be.

Able had pushed the button on the call box again. "I'm not doing the assessment," he'd said. "I have a long drive home. So, please, just bring out the dog."

It was hard to explain. The leaves were so gigantic, and bright as hell. Some had fallen as if they were riding an invisible conveyor belt. Others had spun and flipped the whole way down. Able had started wondering if the monk, on the other end of the call box, had heard what he'd said.

"I appreciate that you've come a long way, Mr. Jones," the monk had said, finally. "But I must insist that you take this last step in the—"

Able had cut him short with a click of the call button. "Bring out the dog," he'd said.

Able didn't know how much we paid for a dog, but he figured it was a lot. And he figured the monk at the other end of the call box didn't know about the money, either. The reason for this, Able suspected, was that the monk in charge of the monastery had always told his subordinate monks that this dog-training business wasn't about the money. In fact, it wasn't even about the dogs. It was about *them*. It was about overcoming their weaknesses as human beings via the dogs.

The call box was silent. Able imagined what was happening. The monk he'd been talking to was going up the monk chain of command, asking had they ever given a dog away without completing the assessment? The monk's boss hadn't known the answer to that question. Neither had his boss's boss. Finally, the call box monk went to talk to the top monk, who knew exactly how much we paid for a dog.

And the top monk had been like, "The man wants his dog, give him his dog."

And the call box monk was like, "But what about the mirror?"

"Pray with me," the top monk had said. Then he'd taken

the call box monk's hands in his. He'd shut his eyes, bowed his head, and said, "Lord, grant me the serenity to accept the things I cannot change . . ."

So the first time Able had seen Mir, the call box monk was walking him on a leash toward the open gate. Mir was happy and looking all around—like he was already downrange, doing his favorite part of the mission, which was mop-up. The monk, on the other hand, appeared to be unhappy. He looked as though he might've been done with all that monk shit.

At the gate, Able had offered, "You want to come with?"

The monk had thought about it while the bells rang, sounding more like a tape recording of bells than actual bells. "No, thank you," the monk had said. Mir, however, had hopped right into the car and sat down on the blanket that Able had spread out for him on the backseat. He was looking at Able like, "Let's fuckin' go."

Able's chair creaked as he sat back down. The room smelled like the stale breath that had carried our words. Chuck leaned into me, as if he were already under the spell of an orange whip. As if the memorial was, for him, spinning. The chaplain began his benediction with "Long ago, the dog ran free."

MIR BLED OUT in the field. Goon, our medic, bagged him. Able wanted to carry him out, but Hal said no. Going forward with the assault, Hal needed everybody's head in the game. He told the breachers to carry Mir. Big Country stopped trilling, pulled back the bolt on his 60, and saw brass. The snipers set out first. Hal followed Able, Big Country followed Hal, and I fell in line. Cutting the last waypoint, we walked directly to the compound. About two hundred meters out, under a bare sissoo tree, Hal told the breachers to lay Mir down. This would've been our fallback position. Meaning, if everything had gone to shit during our raid on the compound, we'd have worked back to this point, and taken stock.

The chaplain told us to go in peace. Outside, we raised our hoods against the shit, and there was Big Country under the lean-to with the dirt bikes. His bags were packed and stacked next to him. We could forgive fear but not the inability to control it; therefore, Big Country was going home in shame. He was boarding a transport that night.

The shuttle that would carry Big Country to the airport was parked nearby. Its doors were locked. Telling me to wait right there, Chuck set off to scare up a driver. He jogged like his knees hurt, out the gate and left, toward a part of the FOB I'd never been to. As I waited, a transport lifted into the sky. The twang of its engines at full power wormed through the night air. It wiggled in the space between me and Big Country. The transport climbed into the shit clouds, leaving a transport-sized dent in the overcast.

It was not hard to predict what would happen to Big Country. He'd go home and be transferred to another unit. Though he wouldn't tell anyone at that new unit what had happened, everyone would know. Big Country would try to reinvent himself, nonetheless. He had the rank to make it to twenty. He had the experience to lead his people into the battlefields of the new century. But every time he told them what he wanted done, or how he thought things should be, they'd think, *He killed one of our own.* And seeing them think that would make Big Country think it, too.

Best case for Big Country, then: his transport would be empty, allowing him to unbuckle at altitude and stand at the center of the cargo bay, where he could imagine himself an actor on a stage. Where the thunder of aerodynamic drag could be his applause, and all the cables, pulleys, and counterweights that rigged the hull would open the curtain on his performance of *Great Circle Route Westward Through Perpetual Night.* Worst case, he'd be surrounded by happy soldiers going home.

ONCE BIG COUNTRY was on his way, Chuck and I walked to Skip's ER. The shit reservoir was nearly empty, the diesel all but burned off. Dying blue flames reflected against the low clouds. Normal clouds formed among the shit clouds.

Skip was a veterinarian. He cared for all military working dogs on the FOB, plus the CIA's horses. Occasionally, he went outside the wire with civil affairs to vaccinate and deworm the GENPOP's livestock. Every once in a while he'd need to bring a sick animal back to base.

Skip's ER, therefore, was equipped with a full surgical suite, including slings, trocars, speculums, and refrigerators full of barnyard IVs. Whether the IVs were tinted orange by some chemical agent or by the sodium lights that hung from the vaulted ceiling, I didn't know. I'd never seen them outside of the place.

Chuck and I entered through a corrugated steel door. It banged shut behind us.

"What'll it be?" Skip asked.

"Three orange whips," Chuck said.

Skip did Chuck first. Chuck's eyes went glassy the instant Skip connected the IV. Maybe even a second before. Then Skip swabbed my arm and pushed the needle into a vein. Crimson blood filled the catheter. The taste of balloon filled my mouth, and the brightness of everything increased. I developed X-ray vision. Thus, I could see through the ER's wall and into the stables. I could see all the way down the shadowy line of stables to the last one. There, a white horse popped its head out. Way back at the beginning of the war, we used to ride these horses, too. We used to dress up in purple cloaks and kufis embroidered in silver. We wore bandoliers full of bullets like golden eggs. Armed with ivory daggers and breech-loading flintlocks, we'd whip our horses to run faster through the darkness. I missed those nights. Meanwhile, Skip swabbed the crook of his own arm. He pushed the needle into his own vein. Reclining into a throne of hay bales, he sighed.

NOT MUCH LATER, we walked along a gravel berm that passed for a road. Light from the streetlamps fell halfway to the ground. Shit rain mixed with real rain.

"Where are we going?" asked Skip.

"To eat," Chuck said.

"Now?" Skip asked, even though we always went to eat after orange whips.

"Yes, now," said Chuck.

Shit cut with water was even slipperier than pure shit. All around us, soldiers clung to one another, so as not to fall. Other soldiers set out on their own in halting steps. They all knew where they wanted to go. Some crouched, teeth bared, eyes slammed shut. Others stood their full height, arms outstretched, as if ready to throw lightning bolts. One soldier slipped and fell, landing hard in shit. Lying on his back, he told the story of a war that had been born to a mother, upon whom he wished a thousand dicks. We walked past him, undaunted. The trick was to walk as if there were no shit at all.

Inside the chow hall, the smell changed from shit to stir-fried garlic. A Korean outfit had won the latest contract, replacing the KBR chefs in their tall white hats. A Korean lady banged her spatula, took orders, and shook ingredients into her wok. Between customers, she wiped the wok clean with a paper towel, then poured in some oil, and steam rose, hissing.

"What you wan'?" she asked Chuck.

Chuck's eyes went from chicken, to shrimp, to meat. "What kind of meat is it?" he asked.

"Meat!" she said.

"No, what *kind*," Chuck said.

"You wan' meat?" she asked.

"Sure," Chuck said.

So Chuck wouldn't be alone, I got meat, too.

"What's in the meat?" Skip asked.

A soldier behind us in line said, "Woof!"

The three of us sat down in the corner, near the stage, where a tuba and a trombone rested on their bells. A clarinet rested on a chair. Skip sat down, shut his eyes, and started to pray. One reason I liked Chuck so much was that he didn't pray, or if he did, he didn't make a big deal about it. He just sat there, not talking, perhaps thinking about his ex-wife, or his Harley back home in Texas, or maybe letting the situation unfold.

The tuba player returned from break wearing his ceremonial uniform, complete with bow tie, cummerbund, and silver braid. We sat before him in our dirty T-shirts and duct-taped boots, with dust in every crack and orifice, our hair slicked back with shit. The tuba player took his seat and lifted his instrument to his lap. The entire population of the chow hall appeared, inverted and blurry, in the polished brass bell.

Skip opened his eyes, looking as if he'd prayed for a tuba player, and there he was.

I forked some meat, cabbage, and a water chestnut, and put it in my mouth. The meat was chewy. Chuck's jaw worked up and down. Skip, who also had a mouthful, flashed a momentary expression of concern.

"Good evening!" yelled the tuba player. He was alone on stage. His medals, awarded for perseverance in the accomplishment of administrative tasks, used to mean something before the war. They jingled as he adjusted himself in his seat. When someone asked him how he got those medals, I wondered, what did he tell them? What did he tell himself? To his credit, he didn't seem to care. He looked happy with his instrument properly balanced and ready to play.

"What do you folks want to hear?" he asked.

Anything, nothing, go fuck yourself.

"All right," said the tuba player. And he started to play.

Remain Over Day

—

Maiwand Valley, Afghanistan

The helicopters left us on a high plateau, in a fog of warm exhaust, late one spring night. They departed, rotors thumping, up and over the mountain on which we stood. A breeze pushed the oily fog off the plateau. Through night vision I watched its warmth tumble downhill, then snag on a patch of sagebrush. The plateau was surfaced in hard, luminous chalk. Hal stepped off its bright edge and into the valley, creating a seam in the night for the rest of us to fold into.

Digger followed Hal, Lex followed Digger, and so on, ducking into that seam, proceeding westward along a narrow footpath lined with sawgrass and wildflowers. Mooch followed Green, who followed Scrape. I watched the patrol stretch into the night, waiting to take my place at the end of the line. Lyle jumped off the plateau like a paratrooper. Goon stepped into the valley behind Lyle. Hank was supposed to go next, followed by Q, then me, but Hank and Q were having an argument. They stood chest to chest by the footpath, exchanging words, and I was too far away to understand why, let alone get there before Hank shoved Q, Q lunged at Hank, and the two men crashed into each other.

Hank and Q were Afghan soldiers, attached to us. But we didn't claim them, necessarily, and they didn't act like ours. Higher had forced them on us at the beginning of the deployment, six weeks prior, in order to make it look like their strategy was working—i.e., the Afghans were standing up while we were standing down. Nine years into the war, however, with no end in sight, we weren't going anywhere. And as far as standing up went, Hank and Q had managed—until that night, at least—to stay out of the way and not cause any trouble.

Locked together, Hank and Q fell off the plateau and rolled downhill, bumping over rocks and crushing knots of sagebrush. Their old Soviet rifles, slung to their chests, clattered like beach chairs. Lasers shone back from the patrol, illuminating the commotion within its own dust cloud. I leapt off the plateau after Hank and Q, while Goon quit the footpath on a diagonal line of pursuit. I tripped over the bullhorn that Hank and Q took turns carrying, and Goon accidentally kicked one of their helmets. The Afghans rolled into a boulder, leaving Q, a hairy, slow-twitch endomorph, on top of Hank, a lanky, fine-boned gatherer of wool.

Q delivered a solid blow to Hank's face, then another. Goon pulled Q off. I helped Hank to his feet.

"Fuckin' idiot," Goon said, shoving Q in the direction of the patrol.

Q's chubby face jiggled in indignation. "Not me," he said.

"Walk," Goon ordered, pointing.

Q picked up his helmet and walked. Goon, muttering curses, fell in behind Q. The patrol started moving again. Hank stood with his head tilted back, trying to control a nosebleed.

I dug a bandanna out of my leg pocket. "Here," I said, offering it to Hank, who, without looking down, reached out a wide, long-fingered hand.

Starlight filled Hank's open palm and cast its shadow on the ground. I relinquished my bandanna and, as Hank's fingers closed on it, I had the odd sensation of having seen Hank's fingers slowly close on my bandanna once before. Not only that, it seemed as though I'd been on this mountain before, on a spring night exactly like this, watching Hank hold the bandanna to his face, hearing blood drip off his elbow and onto a stone.

Wind eased through the wildflowers. I felt each stem bend, every petal rise. I'd experienced déjà vus in the past, but never one this intense. Looking at the ground, for example, I was aware of every rock, pebble, and grain of sand, and I knew how each one had come to be. I sensed every ray of starlight that fell in the valley—on the winding river, on the sleeping cattle—and I could trace each one back in time to its cosmic source. It was a pleasant feeling, understanding how things were put together, not to mention knowing what was going to happen a few seconds before it did. My future self remained dumbstruck in the throes of that déjà vu, deep in enemy territory, as the troop moved farther away. As far as I could tell, however, there was nothing to be afraid of. There was a place for everything, and everything was in its place. But then, without warning, one grain of sand became no different from the next. Stars transformed into nothing special. The déjà vu collapsed, leaving me light-headed and short of breath on the side of that mountain.

Hank stood slightly uphill from me, holding the bullhorn. He looked out from under a purple lump that swelled over one eye.

"Ready?" he asked, like I hadn't answered the first time.

WE PATROLLED WESTWARD along the north side of the river: across dry opium fields whose pods bumped softly against my thighs; through emergent wheat fields whose tillering shoots appeared white-hot on night vision; and over stubbled cornfields clustered with roosting crows. Every now and then I'd stop and look behind myself, to make sure no one was sneaking up. I saw a slinking dog or two. I watched sissoo trees bend in the wind. I considered a glacier, snaking down from the Hindu Kush, glowing like uranium. Turning back toward the patrol, I saw Hal in the distance, standing off to the side.

Whereas everybody else's infrared signature appeared bright and, therefore, a little desperate in the cool night air,

Hal's was muted. Hal ignored Q as Q walked by. He nodded at Goon. He stared Hank down as Hank walked by. Precisely at smile range, Hal smiled at me.

"What happened back there?" he asked, nodding up toward the plateau.

"Hank shoved Q," I said. "Q jumped Hank."

"Then what?"

"Goon and I broke it up."

Hal spoke in a forced whisper, directly into my ear: "I want those fuckheads slapped around when we get back. I want their shit burned and the ashes dumped in their mouths."

We crossed a hard stretch of dirt while Hal stared off into the distance—past Hank, Q, and the rest of the patrol, past where the mountains ended and the valley opened on what the Afghans called "the Kingdom of Sand." Judging by the look on his face, Hal saw something out there that we'd someday have to deal with. For now, though, right in front of us: Q dragged his heels, creating dust clouds, and Hank swayed, causing the tethered lens cap of his night-vision monocle to swing back and forth.

"They'll just send us two more," I said.

"Fuck that," Hal said.

A faraway donkey brayed. The day's heat rose from the ground.

"You say anything to them?" Hal asked.

"No," I said. "You want me to?"

"I should probably do it," Hal said.

"I don't mind," I said.

I stared into the distance, trying to see what Hal saw.

"I think it'd be better coming from me," he said.

It used to be we'd do hard knocks on every raid. We'd creep in under the cover of darkness, position ourselves covertly, and hold very still. A nightingale might chirp, a cow might low, then—*BAM!*—we'd breach the door/hatch/gate, tear through the courtyard/living room/boudoir, and kill whoever needed killing. And if anyone managed to escape, for example, out a back door to run into a wide-open field—tripping over dark furrows, splashing through muddy troughs—I'd call the gunship in from its hiding place in the sky, and it would trip into the field, buzzing, with green light shining out its cockpit windows and blue sparks falling from its engines. Hearing the buzz, the runner would try to pick up the pace only to fall more. I'd mark where he lay in the mud with my laser, drawing green ovals around him as his panic traveled backward through the beam into my hand, up my arm, and into my brain, so I'd feel his hysterical need to get up out of the mud and run. When the runner stood I'd steady the laser between his shoulder blades. The gunship would drop its infrared spotlight—like the magic that turned Cinderella into a princess—on top of the runner, and I'd transmit clearance to fire. Next there'd be a hollow whack, like a suitcase falling onto a baggage carousel, and the shell would appear in the sky, glowing from the friction of aerodynamic drag as it made its slow descent into the field. But those days were over. Higher had decided that the war needed to move in a new direction. After jamming Hank and Q down our throats, they eliminated gunships and hard knocks.

Upon arrival at our first compound, we set up for the call-out. The compound's outer walls formed a square. We lined up along two sides, in a bear-trap formation that hinged on Hal. Hal nodded, and Digger hooked a flash bang over the wall. It landed in the courtyard on the other side with a thump. The fuse cooked for half a second more; then flashes bleached my night vision. Bangs and echoes overlapped. Smoke floated over the wall. Hank raised the bullhorn to his lips to read the statement from memory.

That statement, crafted in English, translated into Pashto, went something like this: "We are coalition forces, committed to the future of Afghanistan. Our presence outside the walls of your domicile, in the middle of the night, should not be construed as a threat to your person, or to the persons you hold dear. Instead, we urge you to look upon this encounter as an opportunity for us to work together, to forge a new bond of cooperation and trust, by which our mutually freedom-loving cultures will prosper."

Hank's reading ended with an electric click, followed by silence. No one from inside the compound offered a rebuttal. No babies cried, no donkeys brayed. No faraway dog barked, *Fuck off!*

Hal kicked down the compound's steel gate with a clang,

and we followed him into the courtyard. We torched a wood-pile, fragged a well, then weaved through an open door. We ran from room to room and found the place vacant. During our search for intelligence, Goon discovered a live hen under a pail. Lex salvaged a bundle of copper wire from a compost heap. I lifted a mildewed tarp and uncovered a laboratory-quality balance scale resting on a splitter log.

The scale's aluminum beam was bright red, its fulcrum made of brass. Starlight pooled in its silver weighing pans. I tapped a finger on one of those pans and the instrument started to seesaw. In its dampening rise and fall I saw the weight of my touch reduced by half, then half again, and so on. Meanwhile, the troop unwound, single file, into the night, folding into that seam that Hal had created. The same seam, I supposed, that he'd created years ago, on our very first mission. Which would explain why it felt so comfortable and safe. It had delivered us this far.

"You coming?" Goon asked. He was standing on the metal gate Hal had kicked down.

I stopped the scale from rocking, and in so doing absorbed the remaining weight of my touch. Stashing the scale in my ruck, I took my place at the end of the patrol.

OUR NEXT COMPOUND was five clicks southwest. Along the way we jumped over a stream like a liquid mirror. We passed a sleeping bull with its eyes squeezed shut and its lower lip hanging down. We crossed soft, dry fields that smelled like medicine. Occasionally, I'd sense the enemy behind me, and, turning around, I wouldn't see him. But as I searched the empty spaces where I thought he might be, I'd feel the approach of another déjà vu, and I'd try to clear my mind in hopes of inducing its onset. I wanted to know how everything came to be again, and I wanted to see, however briefly, into the future. Each déjà vu's approach felt like a whirlpool that I might fall into, but then it would recede, and I'd turn to face the patrol, disappointed. We arrived at our destination around zero two, local.

The second compound's walls were curved. We formed more of a gooseneck than a bear trap around them. Digger had trouble with the pin on the flash bang and wound up tossing it late. It detonated at apogee, lighting our unsuspecting faces.

Q delivered the statement this time, reading off the laminated card that he carried every night, which had delaminated in one corner. At some point water had seeped into that corner, smearing the ink and blurring some of the words. When Q got stuck on those words, Hank would whisper them into Q's ear. Q's repetition of Hank's whispers echoed.

There was no response from inside the walls, again. The compound's gate was made of tree branches lashed together, like a castaway's raft. Hal broke right through it, bodily. We followed him into the courtyard, and under the canopy of an enormous willow. We gained entrance to the rooms via a long passageway with wooden doors on either side. I took the last door on the left and entered an empty room with mud walls, a dirt floor, and another wooden door in the far wall. These doors—fixed with knobs, hinges, and striker plates; hung in what smelled like pinewood frames—fit snugly within the adobe walls. Behind that second door was a third room, with a third door.

Each room I entered was a bit darker and colder than the previous room. My goggles fuzzed like bad reception on the TV. Radio static folded over on itself. I kept thinking that I'd discover something in the next room. I tried to keep my mind open to the possibilities. Like that night I'd found a sextant with its scope, mirror, and graduated arc. Or when I'd stumbled upon that tiny quartz elephant. I'd put those things in my pack and forgotten about them, until weeks later when I was digging around for something to eat. I'd pulled the sextant out of my pack and remembered finding it in a place that had smelled like cinnamon. I recalled a young woman weeping the night I'd discovered the elephant. These rooms, however, were odorless and silent. I left the doors open behind me so that when I turned around, the nearest door framed all the others. I thought maybe I'd find whoever was hanging these doors—a mujahedeen carpenter, if you will, planing the frames to fit just right, oiling the hinges to swing freely. He'd work by candlelight, I imagined, or perhaps he was blind and he'd work by feel. The doors were perfectly balanced and weightless. They seemed to go on forever, which I figured was discovery enough.

———

OUR THIRD AND last compound was three clicks west of the second. We took a meandering path through a sissoo grove to arrive at twilight. The diamond shape of the compound's outer walls fit nicely inside the bear trap. A crooked archway in the southern wall opened onto a shadowed courtyard. Digger was just about to pull the pin on a flash bang and roll it through that archway when a woman exited, carrying an empty pot.

Hank raised the bullhorn and began reading the statement. The woman startled at the noise, then smiled.

Harek, is that you? she interrupted.

Harek was Hank's real name. The woman, it turned out, was his aunt. Moles dotted her narrow face, and her teeth were crooked. Shocked by Hank's battered visage, she touched the purple lump above his eye. She ran her finger over the pink meat of his split lip, which must've stung.

Hank's aunt invited us into her courtyard, where apple trees bloomed and black ants rooted around in the crabgrass. She kept a pigeon in a cage that hung from the branch of a tree. At first, I thought that pigeon was fake—it stood so still, and its feathers were so smooth. But its eyes followed me around the courtyard from the woodpile to the bikes to the buckets. The way the bird stared at me, I felt the need to confess, though to what, I didn't know. I supposed I could've gone down a list of regrets until I hit upon the one that would've made the pigeon look away. Instead, I entered the rooms. In one, two girls slept on the hard dirt floor, their heads touching as if they were Siamese twins. I stayed in that room for a while, listening to the girls breathe, hoping the bird would forget. But as soon as I returned to the courtyard there it was, staring at me with its beady eyes.

WE LEFT HANK'S aunt with aspirin, iodine, and MREs for the girls: Country Captain Chicken, Pound Cake, Sloppy Joe. We wished her peace in her native tongue. From her compound we walked west again, toward the open end of the valley.

The sun had risen over the horizon by then, but the valley remained in shadow. Those shadows appeared striped, like crime scene tape, through night vision. The Kingdom of Sand, off in the distance, shone in golden waves. Putting one foot in front of the other, we searched for a place where the helicopters could pick us up. Meanwhile, Hal radioed dispatch. I listened in on the same frequency. The clerk on the other end told Hal that our signal was "ROD," which was the last thing we wanted to hear after a long night of traipsing around from dry hole to dry hole. It meant that we weren't getting picked up any time soon. It meant: Remain Over Day.

WE FOUND A defensible position at the base of the northern mountains, where there was water from a spring and shade from a tall ash tree. The sun rose higher in the sky, shooting flames in all directions. I sat propped against my ruck. My brain felt heavy, my mind cold. I was gazing up at a cloud when the pale sky around it seemed to flash.

Hal whistled and waved me off my redoubt in the shade. I joined him in the sunny valley. He pointed up toward the western end of the valley's northern mountains, where sunlight fell on a rock formation that resembled dragon's teeth. There, I saw a clear, bright flash.

"You see that?" Hal asked.

The next flash wavered, like sun off an AK's curved magazine.

"See what?" I said.

WE JOKED LIKE we used to when Hal would get some batshit idea and I'd try to talk him out of it. I said, "But we've got no air, no arty, no QRF," meaning quick reaction force, to bail us out of a bad situation.

"Your mom's our QRF," Hal said.

"But they'll see us climbing the mountain, and they'll be ready," I said.

"Ready," Hal chuckled while tightening the laces of his boots. He looked over by the spring, where Hank was filling Q's canteens and Q was dropping iodine into Hank's.

"They seem to be getting along," I said.

"What'd you say to them?" Hal asked.

I pushed fresh lithium cells into my holographic sight.

"Nothing," I said. "I thought you were going to do it."

"No," Hal said.

I thought back to that conversation we'd had on our way to the first compound, as we'd crossed that hard stretch of dirt, and I thought maybe I'd gotten it confused with a different conversation, over some other expanse of dirt.

"So you'll talk to them, then?" Hal asked.

"Sure," I said.

Hal led the patrol uphill while I remained at the base of the mountain, waiting for Hank and Q. Knowing that we were in for a gunfight, the boys were all smiles. Digger shook my hand. Goon hugged me. Lex kissed me on the forehead, leaving the shit smell of his lips behind. Hank and Q tried to walk right past me without saying boo. I stopped them.

"Whatever happened between you two last night can't happen again," I said.

"No," said Q, shaking his head.

"We have enough trouble as it is without having to babysit," I said.

"I am sorry. He is sorry," Hank said.

The purple lump over Hank's eye rolled to one side.

"Don't be sorry, just don't do it again."

Right after I said that, the pigeon popped its head out from under Q's chest plate. Its gray feathers were ruffled. Its short beak was wide open in distress.

"Hello," Q said to the bird.

"You let him steal from your aunt?" I asked Hank.

"Not my aunt. Friend of my aunt," Hank said.

"Whatever," I said. "You need to leave it here."

Q stroked the bird's head with a finger. He said something in Pashto to Hank.

"So you will leave yours here, too?" Hank asked me.

He meant the red balance scale in my pack.

"That's different," I said. "They use scales to make bombs."

"They use birds to lay eggs. They use eggs to stay alive. Alive, they make bombs," Hank said.

"Same," Q said.

"No," I said. "Leave it."

Q left the pigeon on a rock, where it preened its feathers back into place and tucked its stubby wings away. I thought it might hop or glide back down into the valley, but it just stayed on the rock, staring at me as I followed the patrol up the mountain—over soft cascades of sand at first, then little red pebbles that zipped and smoked like matchheads under my boots, then flint. The flint clinked and scraped, and the noise hurt my teeth. Little purple flowers grew in the crags. Snow glittered in the shadows. Near the top of the mountain, the ground smoothed out again. Icy patches of dead grass stood in the shadows of sun-warmed boulders. We moved toward the dragon's teeth like we were back in the States, following a well-worn path to someplace known.

At three hundred meters we shed our packs and drank the last of the water in our canteens. We folded our letters from home along with pictures of our wives, sons, and daughters, and tucked them under rocks so they wouldn't blow away.

From there, we started to leapfrog. Hank and Q leapt with me and Hal. They'd cover us as we advanced, then Hal and I would cover them. We ran into the wind. The sun shone down. Goon, Mooch, Lyle, and the rest leapfrogged on either side of us. To be up and running felt like wearing a suit of bells. Crouching behind a rock, I turned to watch Hank and Q charge past. Hank's good eye was wide open, while Q appeared to be holding his breath. Seconds later, Hal and I sprinted past them, jingling. Thus we closed on the dragon's teeth, until we came to a smooth field of slate.

I could see, across the slate, Taliban peeking through gaps in the teeth. The wind delivered their telltale mix of BO and cigarette smoke. We looked to Hal for the signal—after which we'd run across the slate, firing bursts and lobbing frag—but Hal was staring off into the distance again, at that thing that only he could see. Whatever it was seemed to be telling him to hold steady and let the clouds roll by, then, maybe, broker some sort of truce. Shouting into the wind, we could agree to lay down our arms and meet in the middle. The Taliban could share with us whatever sustained them—smoked knees, fermented milk—and we could cook them an MRE lasagna. Then came the sound of boots on slate. I turned to find Hank, running. Then Q. Then we were all up, howling under the blue sky, running toward the dragon's teeth and whatever lay beyond.

Crossing the River No Name

——

Khost, Afghanistan

One rainy night, in March 2011, we crossed a muddy field to intercept a group of Taliban who'd come out of the mountains of Pakistan. They were walking west. We were patrolling north to arrive at a point ahead of them, where we'd set up an ambush. The field was actually many fields inundated by snowmelt and rain. Piles of rocks, laid by farmers, demarcated the flooded borders. Every so often we'd pass evidence of what had grown in those fields: an island of blighted cornstalks, a soybean shoot—as perfect as a laboratory specimen—floating in a shin-deep lake. Someday, I figured, the sun would come out, the land would dry, and the farmers would be back to restake their claims. That night, however, they'd taken shelter on higher ground, and that entire miserable stretch of Khost was ours.

Electric streaks of rain fell straight down on my night vision. Cold rose from the mud into my bones. It squeezed the warmth out of my heart. My heart became a more sensitive instrument as a result, and I could feel the Taliban out there, lost in the darkness. I could feel them in the distance, losing hope. This was the type of mission that earlier in the war would've been fun: us knowing and seeing, them dumb and blind. Hal, walking point, would've turned around and smiled, like, *Do you believe we're getting paid for this?* And I would've shaken my head, like, *No*. But now Hal hardly turned around. And when he did, it was only to make sure that we were all still behind him, putting one foot in front of the other, bleeding heat, our emerald hearts growing dim.

We made steady progress through the rain until we came to a river. The river looked like a wide section of field that had somehow broken free, that had, for unknown reasons, been set in motion. In fact, the only way to tell river from field was to stare at the river and sense its lugubrious vector. But to stare at the river for too long was to feel as if it were standing still and the field were moving.

Hal called on our best swimmers, Lex and Cooker, to cross first. They removed their helmets and armor. They kept their rifles and pistols. Cooker tied a loop to the end of a hundred feet of rope and clipped the loop to the hard point on Lex's belt. He hooked himself onto the rope behind Lex, and they set off.

Lex and Cooker waded into the icy water. Long waves purled off their knees. Dark voids streamed from their waists. A third of the way across, they lay in the water and sidestroked. Their heads popped up and down on the surface.

Their exhalations wove together in thick paisley clouds. The rope sank and oscillated in the current. Hugs tied on another hundred feet. Lex and Cooker crawled onto the opposite bank—forty yards across, and another twenty downriver— steaming from exertion and cold.

"Pair up," Hal said.

With the rope now anchored at either end, the rest of us would cross wearing all our gear. The first pair—Hugs and Polly—carried the helmets and armor Lex and Cooker had left behind. They clipped themselves to the rope and walked out. Hand over hand, they pulled themselves across the river, then heaved themselves onto the far shore, where they un-clipped and joined the anchor. Hal and I were next. Hal hooked himself to the rope ahead of me and marched out into the river.

As FAR AS I knew, the only thing in the world that scared Hal was water. Which was why he'd joined the navy and become a SEAL—to conquer that fear. And, for the most part, he'd been successful. Ninety-nine times out of a hundred, he was able to overcome his trepidation by sheer force of will. But there remained that one percent, wherein the invincible core of Hal's fear would reassert itself.

The last time I'd seen this happen was September of 2005, on the Atlantic Ocean, in the middle of the night. We'd tracked down a freighter fifteen miles off the coast of Vir-ginia, steaming east. Crouched in our high-speed assault craft, or HSAC, we'd closed in on the massive freighter's starboard quarter, just aft of the island, for a mock raid. It was a training mission; the hijackers on board the freighter were actors, and the rounds in our assault rifles were paint. But everything else was real: the crescent moon, the twenty-foot waves, the darkness between the waves, and the way the moonlight played in their quivering peaks.

The freighter's gigantic engines were throbbing, their heat shining through the thick steel hull. Waves that flattened along the skin of the ship were re-forming perfectly in its wake, as if the freighter weren't there. Meanwhile, Lex, at the HSAC's helm, was bringing us in on a shallow angle, weaving through crests and troughs. Cooker, standing at the bow with the caving ladder hooked to a pole, was raising that pole toward the freighter's bulwarks. At twenty feet and closing, I could hear the hiss of the waves slipping down the freighter's skin. At ten feet, I could hear the sucking sound of wave troughs disappearing under the ship. That was when Hal yelled, "Stop!"

Lex cut the throttles to idle; Cooker retracted the pole. We all lay down in the HSAC, anticipating Hal's call for an emergency breakaway, followed by a banked turn and a high-powered retreat over the waves. Instead, Hal remained silent, allowing us to drift away from the freighter. When I looked up at Hal standing in the HSAC in the moonlight, I saw that his usual infectious calm had been replaced by something more spooky and insular. It was as if he'd realized that our fight against the hijackers of the world would never end, so why continue? Five seconds later, though, he came to his senses. He ordered Lex to chase down the freighter. He directed Cooker to hook the caving ladder onto the bulwarks. And we followed him up the side of the ship, ascending through waves that enveloped us in their cool velocity and threatened to sweep us out to sea.

Later, when I asked Hal what had caused him to yell "Stop!" that night, he said that something hadn't felt right. His answer had seemed credible enough, because nothing ever felt right.

That trek across the slick and forsaken field in Khost, for example. Or my heart's reception of the Taliban's mounting despair. Or the river, whose water smelled like rust, whose current created its own breeze, and whose eddies trapped phosphorescent galaxies of undissolved fertilizer. That river didn't appear on any of our maps. So, to anyone not standing on its ill-defined banks or wading out against its wily current, that river didn't exist. If we were ever going to turn back, this would've been the time.

But I followed Hal into that river—up to my knees and then my waist—to a spot about halfway across, where the current felt stronger at my feet than at my chest. The bottom kept shifting, and a dark crease formed on the river's surface immediately downstream from us. That was where Hal froze.

"We need to move upstream!" I called.

Hal gripped the rope with both hands. "Right!" he shouted, without moving. Then he disappeared below the surface.

Standing my ground, I absorbed Hal's weight on the tightening rope. Then the bottom gave out, and I went under.

It was as if I'd sunk into a well. Still attached to the rope, I bumped into Hal. The current pushed us together, back to back, holding us submerged. We fought to unhook ourselves while the rope twisted. Hal bucked as if he were trying to break out of a straitjacket. His screams were silent, but I felt them in my lungs, and I watched their silver bubbles rise from his mouth.

Times before, when I'd thought I was going to die—like during that ambush in Marjah, on my first deployment, or, two deployments later, when our helo's tail rotor was shot off over Shkin—I'd wanted to cringe at the coming end. Instead, I'd looked to Hal and seen him radiating calm, a calm that had transferred to me so completely that I wouldn't have known the difference had I passed to the other side.

Now Hal had run out of air. He clawed at me in an attempt to propel himself to the surface. In that way, he created enough slack in the rope for me to unclip.

I sank directly to the bottom of the murky hole and kicked off, but fell short of the surface. Sinking again, I drifted downriver. My armor, my weapons, felt weightless in the numbing cold. I floated through Hal's wake: cascades of shear and compression, acceleration and stall. I looked up at the surface, trying not to panic. In a twist of glowing fertilizer, I saw the Virgin Mary.

Doubters, listen: if she can appear at an underpass in Chicago, if she can appear in the bruise on a woman's thigh at an ER in El Paso, then she can appear in a whirlpool of diammonium phosphate, spinning on the surface of an unnamed river in Afghanistan.

Light emanated from her warm, benevolent face. Golden roses lay at her feet. She and I communicated telepathically.

"Am I saved?" I asked, bubbles tickling my lips.

"No," Mary said.

"How come?" I asked.

"Saving you would require a miracle, and you've already used yours," she said, not unkindly.

THE MIRACLE IN question had occurred the morning of Saturday, December 8, 1984, on a football field in Deptford, New Jersey, during a playoff game for the Group III State High School Championship. I was a second-string junior, and not a day had passed since that I hadn't thought about it, or about the events leading up to it, beginning with dinner at Coach D.'s house the night before the game.

Coach D. lived in Ocean City, New Jersey, in a gray duplex on the bay side of the island, between an ice factory and a grass strip, from which banner-towing Cessnas lifted off in summer. He'd grown up in Ocean City, gone to Ocean City High School, played cornerback for the Red Raiders, and been assistant coach for a decade before becoming head coach. "In all that time," Coach D. said, during the speech he delivered over a spread of baked ziti prepared by Mrs. D., "I've never seen a team this good, this bighearted, this brave. Never one as touched by destiny." And with that Coach D.'s voice cracked, and he began to weep.

I had to resist the urge to laugh. I looked away and counted backward from a hundred, so as to avoid insulting a man whose only fault had been to stare failure in the face and carry its weight for the rest of us. Luckily, Maz, our team captain, stepped in and said, "Let's win this one for Coach D.!" And everybody cheered "Coach D.!" in response, over and over.

Amid the ruckus, I laughed without fear of reprisal. Coach D. laughed, too, while wiping away tears. And I took the opportunity to get something else off my chest. To Maz, who was standing ten feet away, I shouted, "I'm in love with your girl!" He didn't hear me. To Gunner, our quarterback, who was standing right next to me, I hollered, "I'm in love with Maz's girl!" Gunner yelled back, "Join the club!" Then the cheering died down, and we ate ziti.

Maz was a fullback, the type who preferred to block so that others might score. He was a born leader and an all-around good guy, the likes of whom I wouldn't encounter again until I met Hal, years later. Maz, like Hal, made me feel as though I was part of something larger than myself. And, like Hal, he made me want to be a better person.

Back then, I had this wooden baseball bat, driven through with heavy nails, that I called the Morningstar. Nights, I'd sneak out the back door of my parents' house on the mainland and carry the Morningstar along fire roads through the Pine Barrens. This was during the casino boom, when new developments seemed to spring up weekly. Finding one, I'd stroll its winding streets, and I'd admire the houses set back in the woods, with moths orbiting porch lights, the smell of wild honeysuckle, and the *tic-tic-tic* of midnight sprinklers. Along the way, I'd pass perfectly good mailbox after perfectly good mailbox.

I'd destroy one of those mailboxes with the Morningstar. Then I'd destroy the next mailbox, and the next. And if, between mailboxes, I came across a parked car, I'd bash its taillights and shatter its windshield. And, at the end of all this, I'd look down the street at what I'd done with some satisfaction, feeling as though I'd put in a good night's work.

The next morning, however, I'd be ashamed. Like the people who I knew were cursing me—waking up to find their mailboxes mangled, their taillights bludgeoned, their windshields caved in—I'd wonder, Who would do such a thing, and why?

Maz's girl was a cheerleader, of course, and, therefore, present at Coach D.'s house the night before the big playoff game in Deptford. Because she'd helped Mrs. D. in the kitchen, I figured she was the one who'd burned the cheese on top of the ziti just the way I liked it. I reckoned that it was some sort of secret communication between the two of us. Imagining what that might mean made the muscles of my jaw seize with desire.

Her name was Natalie, Nat for short. She was wearing a tiny blue dress and white heels.

After the ziti, everyone drifted into the backyard. Coach D. was already out there, jingling change in his pocket, looking up at Cassiopeia. Seeing him lost in thought made me want to laugh again, which made me wonder what the fuck was wrong with me, again. So I turned around and walked the other way, through Coach D.'s house. Right outside the front door, I ran into Nat, standing on the porch with those legs. She looked cold.

"Can you give me a ride home?" she asked.

"Sure," I said.

Nat lived on the north end of the island, in a development called the Gardens, where there were no mailboxes. Where, I supposed, letters and packages floated down under little rainbow parachutes. The Gardens had reflecting pools, lemon groves, and footbridges. It had terraces, verandas, and pavilions. As we drove past these things, Nat seemed not to notice. At a four-way stop, she leaned over and kissed me.

We drove past her house, across the wooden drawbridge at the north end of the island, and onto the sandbar where the

White Deer Motel stood. The eponymous deer, made of cement and painted white, had lost an antler. The room cost ten bucks. The bed was cupped and creased like a fortune-teller's palm. Nat and I spent the next few hours generating what felt like an interstellar transmission. One that explained, via tiny modulations, who we were, what music we liked, what languages we spoke, and all that we knew about the universe up to that point.

We held hands as I drove her home. When I dropped her off, it was still dark. I parked at the far end of the school lot and watched the sun rise from inside my car. Condensation fogged the windshield. I wiped a clear spot so that I could see the locker room door. At six-thirty, Coach D. unlocked that door and propped it open with a dumbbell. Maz's blue pickup arrived a few minutes later, followed by Gunner's Firebird. Soon everybody started showing up. I entered the locker room with the crowd. Inside it was super quiet. I wanted to yell what had happened with Nat. I wanted to shout that love conquers all. Instead, I donned my sour pads and red jersey in silence. I laced my beat-up cleats. And I carried my white helmet onto the bus that would deliver us up the Black Horse Pike to Deptford.

It was a defensive game, as predicted, and scoreless at halftime. At the beginning of the third quarter, Deptford sacked Gunner in the end zone for a safety. With three seconds left in the game the score was still 2–0, Deptford, with us on offense deep in our own territory. Nat was cheering as if this were the most important thing in the world. As if she'd forgotten all about what we'd done the night before. Out on the field, there seemed to be some confusion in our huddle. Maz called a time-out.

Coach D. brought everybody in—offense, defense, special teams, and second string. "Listen to Maz," he said. Maz, crouching at the center of the huddle, talked us through a trick play while drawing arrows in the grass. Looking over the huddle, I saw Nat. She raised a sign with Maz's number written in glitter. She cheered her beautiful fucking head off. I looked past her to the distant end zone. The sun broke through the clouds and shone down on the uprights like something holy.

Seriously, it was like the picture on the cover of a program for the funeral of a kid who'd played football his whole life and loved the game, and died in a tragic accident way too young, and now here you were, stuffed into a coat and tie, sitting in a church pew, looking at that picture, like you were supposed to imagine the dead kid on this field in the sky, scoring touchdowns left and right. Only, the sunbeams shining through the clouds over that football field on that cold Saturday morning in Deptford, New Jersey, in 1984, were real, and I heard the voice of God.

"You want a miracle?" God asked.

The trick-play huddle broke with a loud, sharp clap. Our team took the field. Coach D.'s knees flexed under the weight of our imminent defeat. Nat started to cry.

"Please," I said to God.

"All right," He said. "But just this once."

So it happened. The curtain was pulled back. A giant, heavenly finger poked around among the cogs, and the curtain slid back into place. Some skinny kid, whose name I forget, was sprinting down the sideline, headed for pay dirt. No one was even close. Nat, crying tears of joy, hugged the other cheerleaders, girls whose purity she'd called into question as we'd lain naked at the White Deer. My heart buzzed like a tuning fork. A chubby ref with his whistle in his mouth jogged on a diagonal after the skinny kid, who was still all alone.

"YOU REMEMBER, RIGHT?" the Virgin Mary asked me.

"Of course," I said, a little surprised that she hadn't just read my mind.

Then the Holy Spirit that had infused that twist of undissolved fertilizer on the surface of the river vanished. And, with it, Mary's warmth and light and the golden roses at her feet. I was left to drown, numb with cold, without regrets. Then I bumped into a rock and snagged on another. I crawled onto the river's far shore, and I was saved.

Lex splashed up to me. "Shh," he said, because I was heaving loudly, and we were close, theoretically, to the Taliban patrol. Lex whispered into his radio, "It's F.S.," which stood for Fuckstick, which was what Hal called me, usually just joking around. "He's okay."

Lex splashed away, downriver. I stood, readjusted my

goggles, and saw what was happening: my teammates on either side of the river, anchoring the rope. Others in the river, hooked to the rope, diving and surfacing. Still others walking up and down the banks with their rifles pointed at the surface, sparkling creases, eddies, and points where the dark water parted around rocks. Hal must've unclipped, too.

I turned to face the field, which was no less shitty on that side of the river, though the rain had stopped. My goggles clicked and whirred, trying to bring the darkness into focus. I walked into that darkness, half-expecting to find Hal walking the other way. Like he had that night in Marjah, after we'd been separated by the ambush. Or that day in Arizona, during our HALO refresher, when nobody'd seen his chute open, and we were all looking in the sagebrush on the windward side of the drop zone for his body, and he'd popped out the leeward side, carrying his chute like a pile of laundry. Eventually, I stopped walking and just stood in the mud, allowing its cold to rise into me.

I felt the Taliban out there still, their hearts transmitting something more elemental than despair. Something more akin to chaos.

Digger took over in Hal's absence. I heard him, over the radio, making the report back to Higher.

"Roger," Higher said.

That's it? I thought. Fucking *Roger*?

I wanted to get on the radio and tell Higher that a guy like Hal doesn't just fall in a river and die. But then I was afraid that saying those words might make them true. Perhaps that was why Higher hadn't said anything, either. We were in this gray area, status-wise, where nobody'd thrown out an MIA or a DUSTWUN. Where no one at Higher had directed anyone to open Hal's dead letter to figure out where his next of kin were and what their wishes might be, as far as notification went. Hal's ex-wife, Jean, for example—at her desk on the third floor of the insurance building—who wanted her dad to break the news. Or Hal's son, Max, in high school, in an unidentified classroom, with or without the friends he might have wanted by his side. The letter containing that information remained sealed in a box, with everyone else's.

"Say intentions," Higher asked Digger.

As Digger considered his options, it started raining again, in reverse it seemed, as if the rain were coming up from the ground to fill the clouds.

"I'm gonna leave a squad here to search and take the rest to intercept," Digger radioed back.

I was relieved when Digger put me on the intercept. The river was dizzying, even with my back to it. I wanted to distance myself. I wanted to make it a thing I could look back on.

Digger called Lex, whom he was leaving in charge of the rescue effort. Lex looked at Digger like he used to look at Hal. Like he didn't know what came next.

"Let me know," Digger said.

Then we walked away from the river, northbound. The

sounds of the rescue, already quiet, fell away, and the heat signatures of the rescuers dimmed. Soon enough, behind us was no different from in front of us. The clouds refused to break. Rain wired the air in bright filaments.

The Taliban appeared in the east, at first, as a low cluster of stars. Then as phantoms. Then as men with heat rising off their backs like creeping flames. They walked in a shapeless formation, bunching up and stretching out, because they couldn't see one another. They couldn't see themselves.

All we had to do was stand perfectly still, in a line parallel to their direction of movement, at a range of no more than thirty yards, and wait for them to walk right in front of us. Then wait for Digger's sparkle, which would be our signal to open fire.

This wasn't our first time running an intercept on a Taliban patrol across a muddy field at night. In fact, it was our seventh. During the course of our previous six intercepts, we'd developed and refined this tactic. The enemy would walk right in front of us, and Hal would choose one man. Not the leader, he had explained, whose mind had been made up. And not the dumbass in the back, either, who'd never know any better. But a man in the middle. A man who understood what was happening well enough to have doubts. A man who, having walked this far through darkness, cold, and rain, was no longer sure where he ended and the night began.

Such confusion registered on night vision. When Hal found this man, he'd light him up with sparkle. The man wouldn't know, because sparkle was infrared; it operated on a frequency that the naked eye couldn't detect. So, as far as Hal's chosen man or any of the other Taliban knew, they were still walking in the dark. They were still on their way to their destination. Meanwhile, Hal's sparkle would reflect off the man's wide-open eyes and shine back out like some special knowledge.

That would be the man we'd spare. And that would be the man who'd drop to his knees in the mud and, in a cloud of gun smoke, raise his hands in surrender. That would be the man who'd tell us who he was, where he'd come from, and why.

The Fire Truck

—

I parked in front of the microwave antenna at the top of Craner Peak. A cold wind blew from the east. The warm sun floated overhead. Reed dropped the tailgate. We pulled the hard cases from the bed of the pickup. We shouldered our packs. We'd been home from Afghanistan just two months and already the pack that I'd worn there—the one that had become an extension of me—now felt like somebody else's. Puffy white clouds dragged across the sky. Smooth rocks studded the domelike crest of the mountain. Reed and I carried the equipment over that crest, toward a footpath that wound down the mountain's eastern face.

The snowcapped Wasatch Range came into view first, followed by Salt Lake City and the Great Salt Lake. The bombing range was in the sand between the western shore of the lake and the base of Craner Peak. The observation point, or OP, from which we'd control the jets that would drop the bombs, was a stone outcropping at the top of a steep draw.

Arriving at the OP, Reed and I lowered the hard cases. We slid out of our backpacks. I stepped to the edge of the outcropping and looked down upon the live impact zone.

A thousand feet below, atop a smooth field of sand, was a bright red fire truck.

"That doesn't look right," I said.

Actually, it looked like the fire truck had been trying to reach the center of the impact zone. As if, perhaps, there'd been a fire there, and in their haste to save the day, the firemen had driven off the hardened access road and gotten bogged down in the sand. They'd need a crane to lift it out.

"Anybody down there?" Reed asked.

Through the binoculars, I saw a set of boot tracks walking from the driver's-side door back toward the access road.

"No," I said.

Reed stuck his fingers in his mouth and whistled the way one might to hail a passing cab, or to turn a wayward dog. It was a bright, clean sound that seemed to penetrate everything and pull it slightly apart. Thus, the shadowed crags in the rocky draw, the silver horns on the white roof of the fire truck's cab, the deep jade swirl at the center of the Great Salt Lake, all seemed to waver. I felt this instability in my heart, even, like it was foaming. If anybody was down on the impact zone, they would've felt it, too. They would've emerged from wherever they were hiding and raised their blank faces toward the OP.

Reed stopped whistling and the world stabilized. The fissure in my heart sealed. Nobody appeared on the impact zone.

"Maybe we should call Oasis," Reed said.

"Worth a try," I said.

Oasis was the radio call sign of the Utah Test and Training Range's security force, whose primary responsibility was to protect the top secret laboratory located somewhere in the vast desert west of Craner. That lab was rumored to house extraterrestrials. Therefore, I imagined it to be a town like any other, with parades, baseball games, and fireworks on the Fourth of July, where extraterrestrials and human beings lived as one. Where the aliens taught us how to conquer entropy, and we taught them how to love. Such a place would require the strictest protection, which didn't leave Oasis much time to manage the bombing ranges.

Reed removed the radio from his pack, powered it up, and tuned it to the proper frequency. "Oasis, this is Bulldog," Reed broadcast.

Ten watts emanated off the radio's omnidirectional antenna. Some of that energy descended into the draw, tumbled off the rocks, and spilled out over the lake. Some of it shot up into the sky, wormed its way through the ozone, and forged a path to infinity. Still more hopped Craner Peak, behind us, carrying Reed's transmission over fields of warm sagebrush to a cinder-block waystation, where, en route to the range earlier that day, Reed and I had stopped to register with Oasis.

A counter spanned the linoleum width of that waystation. A guard wearing a stiff comb-over rested his elbows on it.

Behind the guard were racks of shotguns, computers, radios, and closed-circuit televisions. Though the guard hadn't looked busy, Reed and I had waited behind the sign that said, WAIT HERE. The guard had watched us as if through a one-way mirror.

Having received no reply to his first transmission, Reed keyed the mike again. His voice must've emanated from one of the radios behind the waystation guard. "Oasis, this is Bulldog. How do you hear?"

"Go ahead, Bulldog," the guard replied.

"I'm standing on the OP, looking down at a fire truck on the impact zone. I'm wondering if it's supposed to be there."

"If it's on the impact zone, then it's a target," the guard said.

"This doesn't look like a target, is all. It's got its windshield, still, and hoses. And it looks like it drove out there under its own power."

The guard must've looked over his shoulder at the closed-circuit TV labeled CRANER. He must've seen the wave of sand piled up in front of the fire truck's chrome bumper.

"Let me make a phone call."

Radio static hissed as a tall white cloud passed by. Fossils cast in the stone outcropping resembled harpsichords and brains.

"They're telling me that the fire truck is a target," the guard said.

"Who's telling you that?" Reed said.

"My supervisor, Bill."

Maybe Bill was the type to understand how at any given moment a thing could be both target and nontarget. How the more you tried to nail it down one way or the other, the less known it would become. But chances were slim.

"I can have Bill call you if you want," the guard offered.

"That's okay," Reed said.

"All right, then."

Reed and I went through our setup routine. Opening the hard cases released the smell of ozone. We removed each piece of equipment from its foam rubber bed. We warmed the lasers, synced the clocks. We stabilized the coordinate generators. Ready, the equipment clicked and whirred. The radios whispered, *Hush*. Down on the sand, the fire truck shone in the sun. We waited for the jets.

I lay back on the outcropping. The stone was warm, the breeze refreshing. Sunshine penetrated my eyelids, soaking through my retinas and into my mind, where it turned all my memories blue.

The voice of the lead pilot over the radio snapped me out of it: "Bulldog, Widow One Five."

The air base from which the jets launched was north of Salt Lake City. Searching the sky in that direction, I detected a slip of vertical motion. Then the jet came out of afterburner, leaving a tall column of black smoke. I watched the jet climb up and over the city. The sun flashed off its canopy as it rolled inverted and pulled toward the range. A second jet rose from ammering air base, then a third. Each jet carried four hundred-pound laser-guided bombs.

I manned the laser designator. Searching through the scope, I found the levers of the fire truck's pump control station, and the dials above the levers with their needles all at zero. I found an axe, hanging below a pike, hanging below a section of hard hose. I saw Craner's rocky base reflected in the fire truck's windshield before I found the three silver horns on the roof of the cab. Reed manned the radio.

"Say when ready for talk-on," Reed transmitted.

"Go ahead," the pilot answered.

A talk-on oriented the pilot to the target environment. It began by identifying something large and obvious, then proceeded in a narrowing line toward the target. The pilot would follow along either by looking outside, with the naked eye, or by looking through a camera that was mounted to a targeting pod that hung on a wing.

Reed began his talk-on with the Great Salt Lake and its dark green center. Next, he described a spot along the lake's western shore where sand and water twisted into a yin-yang.

"What's a yin-yang?" the pilot asked.

From there, Reed moved west again, focusing the pilot's attention onto the sand at the bottom of the draw, where the shadows of two clouds combined to form what looked like a devil's head.

"Got it," the pilot said.

Reed asked, "What do you see between the devil's horns?"

"A fire truck," the pilot answered.

"That's your target," Reed said.

Reed stacked the jets in a counterclockwise orbit out [of] the lake. The first jet rolled wings level and dove toward t[he] target. Reed cleared him to drop. I triggered the laser. The air horns created a nice refraction, which the bomb steered toward by means of adjustable fins. The fins banged up and down against their stops, causing the bomb to fall through the air like a shuttle through a loom, also causing it to chatter. Looking through the designator's scope at the silver horns, I listened to the falling bomb. I watched the fireball silently blossom, right over the horns. The bang rolled up the draw to reach me with torn edges. The heat warmed my face.

The fire truck steamed as if it had been broiled. A blue halo of shattered glass surrounded it. Levers on the pump control station that had been up were down, and vice versa. Otherwise it looked fine.

More jets arrived to circle high in the stack, as others corkscrewed down into the chute. There was a long period of direct hits in which nothing seemed to change. Where some core thing held together, blast after blast. Which made me wonder if I should stop the bombing, call in a crane, and tow the fire truck to the laboratory, and down Main Street to the center of town, where the fire station would've been had they still needed one. Meaning, had the aliens not yet taught the humans how to inoculate themselves against pyromania, or other acts of god. I thought maybe the aliens and humans could work to-

restore the fire truck back to its original condition, so
uld drive it down the street during their parade. Then
thing vital broke open down on the live impact zone.
y smoke poured from a deep fissure in the fire truck's hull.
he cab tore open, the doors blew off, the seats ejected, the
front axle collapsed. Chrome boiled, and the red finish melted.
I shone the laser on whatever I could find through the billow-
ing smoke: intake cowling, engine block, drive train. It wasn't
long before all that remained was the pump.

The iron pump looked like two elbows locked together. I
shot the laser into one open flange, and the refraction bloomed
out another. The pump gonged under the weight of two,
three, and four bombs. It cracked under the weight of a fifth.
The last bomb tore it open. A brass impeller paddle-wheeled
out of the fireball, pulling flames with it. The impeller's blades
separated in midair, sailing off to leave deep maroon scars in
the sand.

Coming off target, the jet flew right over Reed and me on
the OP. It was such a strange sight: the jet, knife-edged, maybe
thirty feet off the ground. It was so close I saw every panel in
the fuselage, and every rivet in every panel. The pilot looked
right at me. It was like she stood on one side of a bottomless
crevasse, and I on the other. But she was weightless. I saw her
eyes behind her dark visor. I saw her pencil, dummy-corded
to her kneeboard, floating in mid-cockpit. I saw her French
braid rising off her shoulder toward her canopy. Then she
was gone, and the mountain shook in her wake.

Yankee Two

Hit, Iraq

It glowed blue under the new moon. We walked toward it from the south—across the rocky desert, over railroad tracks and a four-lane highway, then down a dirt road that ran perpendicular to the silver Euphrates. We took our third left onto a paved street. Our target building had sliding windows and a muddy garden out front. J.J. darkened the flickering streetlight across from it with one suppressed round—*thhp, dink*—and pieces of glass tumbled to the earth. We took positions for the raid—security in the back alley; blocking stations on the intersections to the east and west; assaulters on both sides of the front door—and waited for Spot.

If Spot had thought everything was cool, he would've given J.J. a thumbs-up. Instead, Spot hurried over to the assaulters on the door. He grabbed Mike by the sleeve and swapped him with Tull. He grabbed Tull and swapped him with Zsa-Zsa. He sent Bobby to the back alley to link up with Lou. Spot had never done so much shuffling around, but this

ght after Qa'im, and we were all still a little uneasy.
epped back from the door—if not satisfied with the
es he'd made, then at least willing to give this new con-
ration a try. He looked at me, standing off the corner of
e building, where I always stood.

I wanted to make eye contact with Spot so he could see
that I was okay. I knew how to look okay. I knew how to
make it seem like I wasn't bothered by what had happened at
Qa'im—or, for that matter, at Habbaniyah or Ramadi. The
funny thing was, nothing had happened at any of those
places. Nothing bad, at least. At Qa'im, we'd been ambushed,
caught with our pants down. But we'd managed to fight our
way out. And we'd killed a lot of insurgents along the way.
Insurgents who were ex–Republican Guard, or Saddam's version of us. Yet no one in our troop was even hurt—unless you
count Lou, who either didn't feel pain or did an excellent job
fooling himself. No one could argue, however, that bad nights
didn't happen, and that we weren't due for one.

Standing outside that building in Hit, I tried not to think
about it. I tried to act like everything was fine, and I wanted
to see myself reflected in Spot's gaze.

The problem was, Spot had a lazy eye, and I always mixed
up which one. After figuring it out, I'd tell myself "left is
right" or "right is wrong," to improve my chances of remembering the next time. Inevitably, though, I'd look directly into
Spot's bad eye. That night, his misalignment skewed toward
the Pleiades, or that part of the sky where Zeus had trans-

formed the seven daughters of Atlas into doves, t⸺
doves into stars. Before I could correct myself, Spot⸺
toward the street and gave J.J. a thumbs-up.

J.J., standing under the darkened streetlight, was an
smoker who would've lapsed during times like this but for
cigarette's telltale glow. Still, he eased his nerves pretending.
By his pantomime I knew that he'd held his cigarette between
his ring and middle fingers, flicking the ash with a card-trick
action of his thumb. His whole hand had covered his mouth
as he'd brought the filter to his lips and inhaled. That night,
in late March, his exhalation was warm enough, or the air
cold enough, to create what appeared to be smoke.

J.J. gave the signal, Mike kicked open the door, and the
assaulters funneled in. I remained outside, watching the alley
between the target building and its eastern neighbor, while
Spot kept an eye on the western alley. A trickle of sewage ran
out of my alley and into the street. Or was it gasoline? Our
target building in Qa'im had been booby-trapped with gas
cans duct-taped with nails. Former members of Saddam's Republican Guard had waited for the assaulters to get far
enough inside before triggering the explosions via remote
control. But this smelled more like shit. Or did it? As the assaulters ran though the building, I debated whether or not to
break radio silence to warn them about something that might
turn out to be nothing. Zsa-Zsa beat me to it.

"The refrigerator is padlocked," he broadcast over troop
common from the kitchen.

...med in from a bedroom on the second deck: "The
...d ceiling are mirrored."

...en Bobby, from the back alley: "I got a car up on
...ks." These observations tended to snowball.

"Shut your fucking traps," Spot told everyone on that frequency.

The remainder of the assault passed in silence, and the
search for intelligence began. Spot sent me in. I ran through
the front door and into the living room, where I flipped cush-
ions off the couch. As a tech, I was looking for phones, SIM
cards, flash drives, and those same things disguised as, or hidden within, something else. I worked by the red light of my
headlamp. The TV remote was just that; the clock radio on
the kitchen counter flashed midnight or noon; the refrigerator
was indeed padlocked. I opened it with bolt cutters and
dipped my hand into every cold pail of cream. Moving on, I
lifted the lid on every dented teapot. I dug my knife into the
flour jar, the sugar bowl. I climbed the stairs to the second
floor. There I found Tull staring at a Big Wheel parked in the
hall. I continued up the stairs to the third floor. Mike stood in
a doorway.

"C'mere," he whispered.

I followed Mike into a room with an open window. A boy
sat on his bed.

"I need to go up on the roof," Mike said. "Can you keep
an eye on him?"

"Sure," I said.

The boy's bare chest was congenitally sunken. ... chattered. Blue night creeping in the window mixed v... red glow of my headlamp to render him purple. I knev... Arabic word for "stand." The boy stood. His pajama t... toms were printed with soccer balls. I patted them dow... and squished the pockets. The boy was clean. I told him, in English, to sit back down on his bed, which he did. I showed him how to lace his fingers together and rest his hands on top of his head. We looked at each other, both of us with our fingers laced, hands on top of our heads. I told him to stay just like that.

I found a computer hidden under a blanket beneath the boy's desk. I removed the blanket and set the computer on top of the desk. It was a work in progress, a kludge of salvaged components, and quite possibly an innocent hobby, though I wouldn't know for sure until I'd taken the hard drive back to the lab, for analysis.

The boy had mounted a SATA drive on a fourteen-inch aluminum rack, along with a 480-watt power supply. He'd used eight billion of these itty-bitty fucking screws. I removed my micro tool set from my side pocket. Opening its plastic case released the smell of the lab—a mix of acetone and ozone that never failed to calm me. I began unscrewing the world's tiniest screws with the world's tiniest screwdriver.

Meanwhile, the rest of the troop was wrapping things up. They slipped past the boy's room. They crept down the stairs. They lined up in the street, ready to leave. Approximately screws remained. I decided to break the drive off

. I bent it up, hard as I could. I pushed it down, same.

it up again, this time harder, harder—

BANG!

I thought the door to the boy's room had slammed shut. But I turned to find Mike in the doorway, smoke rising from his chamber. The boy, still sitting on the bed, looked unhurt. His eyes were wide open, his arms straight up. There was a chip in the cinder-block wall behind him, high and right. Mike didn't take a second shot, as we were trained to. As was, by then, all but reflexive. He just penetrated the room with his eyes down his sights, and reached into one of the boy's pajama pockets.

"He's clean," I said.

But Mike pulled something out. He flipped it over in his hand. It was a black box the size of a deck of cards. Mike looked for switches, wires, antennas—anything to indicate that it might transmit a signal, activate a fuse, detonate explosives, and bring the whole building down on our heads.

Spot appeared, bottom lip packed with chew, lazy eye twitching. Taking the box from Mike, he performed his own inspection.

"He was digging in his pocket for it," Mike said.

Spot held the box at arm's length. "You think it's a trigger?" he asked me.

Triggers were walkie-talkies, cordless phones, and garage door openers.

"No," I said.

The three of us turned our headlamps on the [
arms, which had lowered maybe half an inch, shot bac
revealing curls of pit hair. Shadow filled the depression in
chest.

"What is this?" Spot asked in his rinky-dink Arabic.

The boy shrugged.

"Get him some shoes," Spot said.

I KNOTTED THE elastic so the hood would stay on the boy's
face. I looped the zip ties back around so he couldn't work his
hands free. He was twelve, maybe thirteen. Right at the lower
end of what we considered fighting age. In his closet were a
pair of sneakers with light-up soles, and loafers decorated
with brass buckles. I led him out of his room, in the loafers,
and onto the stairs, down which he moved like he'd never
descended a flight of stairs. I steered him out the front door
and across the muddy garden of trampled dandelions. Holding the boy by the arm, I took my place among the troop
lined up along the curb.

J.J. signaled, *Move,* and Zsa-Zsa stepped off on point.
Bobby stepped off ten yards behind Zsa-Zsa. Lou waited for
Bobby to walk his ten yards. Meanwhile, Bobby stared at a
storm drain on the other side of the street. A dull glow, visible
on night vision, emanated from the grate. It could've just
been heat rising off the sewage below, but then again, it
could've been something else. Something that might climb up

⸺eet and end our unusual streak of good luck. The
⸺ged, Bobby raised his rifle, and I tightened my grip
⸺boy's upper arm. I felt his pulse quicken. Closing on
⸺torm drain, Bobby hit it with sparkle.

We each had a device mounted to our rifles that generated
sparkle—i.e., an infrared spotlight with a laser at its center.
We used it to illuminate targets, and to see into dark places
we otherwise couldn't. Bobby's infrared spotlight, for example, brightened the depths of the storm drain. His laser
skipped across its heavy iron grate. Below the grate, shadows
opened and closed like doors. Waves appeared in the infrared
beam, diverging from the laser like ripples from a stone
dropped in a lake. Which was the opposite of what I'd observed the night before, in Qa'im.

Our target building in Qa'im was like a cubist interpreta-
tion of a target building: its cinder blocks were stacked pre-
cariously; its windows appeared to be an assembly of
fractured windows. After the gas cans blew—further destabi-
lizing the walls and shattering the windows for good—small-
arms fire rained down from adjacent buildings.

I was standing off the corner of the target building, waiting for Spot to send me in, when the ambush triggered. I took
cover in an alley overgrown with ragweed. By the sound of
the onslaught—AKs clattering, RPGs whistling in—we were
surrounded and outnumbered. Any second, I figured, the
enemy would press his attack. Rounds hit short, spraying
dirt. Gunmen shouted to one another, roof to roof. Some-

thing moved in the alley across the street. I spar_
there was Spot with my laser on his chest. Infrared
converged, as if Spot were drawing energy from the c_
block wall he leaned against, the ragweed that partially c_
cealed him, and the cool night air above. Seeing me, Spo_
signaled, *Come.*

Spot covered me as I ran across the street. Glass crunched
underfoot. Bullets ricocheted off the pavement. I ducked into
the alley and leaned against the wall opposite Spot. I remained
standing and fired one way while Spot knelt and fired the
other. I felt his rounds zip past my abdomen. Smoke poured
from the broken windows of the target building. The enemy's
rooftop shouts grew anxious. Spot and I fell into an on-and-
off rhythm, like men working on the railroad. Our rifles
clanged like two sledgehammers striking the same metal
spike. I either killed a dude on a roof or he ducked down in
the nick of time. A door opened up the street from the target
building, and J.J. appeared.

I covered Spot as he ran to J.J. Spot and J.J. covered me. I
followed them through the door and into a living room. The
three of us vaulted a couch. We crashed into a kitchen that
smelled like meat about to turn. A woman, upstairs, screamed.
Spot reached to open the back door and an RPG detonated in
the living room behind us. Firelight illuminated the kitchen. I
could see in J.J.'s and Spot's faces that we might not make it.
Both of Spot's eyes were fixed on the same point. He counted,
One, two, three, then flung open the back door. We ran into

ring at windows, doorways, and shadows on all

w Hit was shaping up to be something of a milk run.
o I thought until I saw the infrared waves, in Bobby's
arkle, reversed. Did waves diverging from the laser mean
hat we were fucked? Or was it waves converging, à la Qa'im?
Had we, in fact, been fucked at Qa'im? It could've been so
much worse. Lou had taken a nail in the thigh, which he'd
yanked out with a pair of pliers on the helicopter ride back to
the outpost. He'd held up the nail, bent and bloody, for all to
see, before chucking it out the helo's open ramp, into the
night.

Bobby stopped sparkling the storm drain and continued
walking up the street. Lou, not even limping, stepped off behind Bobby. It was uphill, maybe a quarter mile, to the intersection where we'd turn south toward the highway, the
railroad tracks, and the desert beyond. J.J., still standing
under the shot-out streetlight, took another drag of his imaginary cigarette. Then, all at once: Lou sparkled a pile of trash;
Zsa-Zsa sparkled a bedsheet hanging from a rooftop clothes-
line; and Tull sparkled a ground-floor window, making it
surge like a portal to another dimension.

"This ain't *Dark Side of the fuckin' Moon* laser light
show!" Spot radioed, and all the sparkles went dark.

SUNRISE, BACK AT our outpost: decelerating rotor blades
cast zoetrope shadows on the LZ. The pilots unstrapped, the

gunners folded belts of 7.62 into ammo cans, and walked toward the huts. I unassed the trail helicopt assisted the boy in the same way I'd assisted him fro curb outside his home, through the streets of Hit, acr the highway and railroad tracks, and into the desert, wher the helos had picked us up. Now I guided the boy, still hooded and zip-tied, to crouch under the dipping rotor blades. We met J.J., Spot, and Mike beside the twisted and rusty hatch of a bombed-out ammo dump.

"You seen him fucking around in his pockets?" J.J. asked me.

Spot held the box, which was somehow blacker in day-light.

"No," I said. "I was taking his computer apart."

"Little something called situational awareness," Spot said. "Heard of it?"

Spot's bad eye stared directly into the sun. He handed me the black box to take back to the lab.

"And what the fuck happened with you?" J.J. asked Mike.

"I missed," Mike said.

"Then what?" Spot asked.

"His hands were up," Mike said.

The wind blew, the ammo dump's rusty door creaked on its hinges, and I saw inside. Sunlight slanted through multiple bomb holes in the roof.

Spot said to J.J., "I guess we shoot once, then wait to see if the target's had a change of heart."

s so," J.J. said.

. the ammo dump I escorted the boy north along the

t's only road. Plywood huts lined either side. We passed

and J.J.'s hut, Lou and Mike's. We yielded to Zsa-Zsa, in

s silk robe, on the way to the shower. We sidestepped the

tractor tire that Tull liked to flip end over end while working

on his core.

I didn't pull on the boy's arm, and he didn't try to break free. He just put one foot in front of the other, as he had for the entire journey from Hit, moving not too fast and not too slow. And never once had he veered off course, even during that long stretch across the desert when I'd let go of his arm. Where any other detainee would've booked it and I would've had to chase him down, the boy had simply walked right alongside me, hooded and handcuffed, the brass buckles on his loafers flashing in the starlight.

The boy was, without a doubt, the most cooperative detainee I'd ever had to walk out of anywhere. After we'd reached the pickup zone—a hard patch of dirt three miles west of Hit—I'd sat him down on the most comfortable rock I could find. I'd given him fresh water and pound cake from my escape-and-evade stash. I'd even thought about calling the terp over to help me explain to the boy what was about to happen, right before it happened.

The helicopters had dropped out of the sky with a hellacious screech. We were sandblasted, mercilessly. The boy had

panicked and tried to run, and though I couldn't bl[...]
I couldn't let that happen, either. So I'd dragged him
the spinning rotors, kicking and writhing, as sand got i[...]
eyes and tears rolled up my face. I'd tossed him into the b[...]
like a bale of hay. Then I'd jumped on top of the boy so h[...]
wouldn't slide out the open door as the helo made a climbing
turn toward the outpost.

Once we were level and headed southwest, I'd propped
the boy up against the cockpit firewall, facing aft. I'd sat at
his feet with my legs hanging out the door. I'd watched the
sun rise and daybreak brighten the face of the boy's hood.
Power lines had flashed below the helicopter's skids. Goats
had run in counterclockwise circles in their pens. Above, a
flock of cranes, scared by the helicopters' noise, had tucked
their wings and dive-bombed us, missing the rotors by inches.

At the north end of the outpost's solitary road was the
Facility, where we kept the detainees, though not for long.
Just a day or two, usually, or whatever time it took to run a
few interrogations. Those who we considered guilty were
transferred to a higher-level institution outside Baghdad.
Those who we deemed innocent we'd drive east to within
walking distance of the highway; then we'd release them with
as much water as they wanted to carry, and twenty bucks so
they might negotiate a ride home. Those men must've told
their stories, which must've been repeated by others, which
meant that the boy might've heard them. Which meant that

ve known about the helicopter ride and the walk
is straight, dusty road. He might've also heard that at
d of the road, we'd climb three stairs and enter a stuffy
n that smelled like bleach. Now we stood in the Facility's
bby. The door banged shut behind us, and the boy jumped.

"Check-in!" I yelled through the wool blanket that separated the lobby from the cells.

Five detainees—most of whom I'd walked out of one
place or another, all of whom had been with us since before
Qa'im—knew what "check-in" meant. They started hissing
their ventriloquist hiss, a neither-here-nor-there sound that
served as both a means of communication and a form of resistance. Here, the hiss was meant to welcome the boy, while
also letting him know that he wasn't alone. Its message was
unmistakable. Soon enough the boy would be practicing in
his cell—projecting his hiss across the room at first, then
through the wall, then around the corner and into the future.
So that years from then, after the war was over and I was
home for good, I'd lie awake next to my sleeping wife, with
our children dreaming in their own beds, and I'd hear it.

"Hello!" I yelled over the hissing.

The interrogators, O. Positive and R. H. Negative,
emerged through the wool blanket. They took in the boy's
pajamas, loafers, and overall scrawniness.

"Little young, don't you think?" R.H. said.

"Yankee Two likes 'em young," O.P. said, referring to me
by my radio call sign.

"He was acting funny," I said. "But I don't tl.
bad."

"They're all bad," O.P. said.

I heard a hiss right behind me, but I knew better than
turn around.

"What'd you find on him?" R.H. asked.

I produced the black box. O.P. took it out of my hand to
see that it had no headphone jack, no speaker/mike, no charge
port. He discovered, as well, that the black box weighed more
than expected. And he might've noticed, furthermore, the
harmony of its rectangular dimensions. Which, I'd later learn,
obeyed the golden section; that is to say, side A was to side B
as B was to the sum of A and B.

O.P. returned the black box to me and said, "If that thing
ain't bad, then I'm Mother Teresa."

THE ICE MAKER had been a Christmas gift addressed to ANY
SOLDIER. Positioned on the floor next to my cot, it played a
lullaby. The tap rolled open, water poured from the tank into
the freeze tray, and the heat exchanger kicked on. This was
just a loop of copper pumped with Freon, but it purred loudly
enough to drown out any tire flipping, forklifts, or mortar
attacks outside. Days the interrogators played the crying
baby tape over and over, it muffled the cooing, fussiness, even
the screams at the end. The water froze, and a stainless steel
auger turned to break the ice into half-moons. The ice slid
down a chute and rumbled into the hopper. After several cy-

...opper was full. The machine beeped softly, and its
...t blinked.

...arried the hopper, full of ice, through the wool blanket
... separated the sleeping area from the lab. The clock on
...e wall said eight. Starlight shone through the seams of my
hut. The black box and the hard drive were on the work-
bench, where I'd left them before I'd gone to bed, around five.
The hard drive, I'd discovered, was blank. Scattered about
were all the tools I'd used to test the black box: gausser/
degausser, car battery, jumper cables, acid bath, sledge. There
was the jammer that I'd used to radiate the black box, hoping
to elicit some response. All of those tests were negative.

Now I carried the hopper outside, under the clear night
sky. The tiniest sliver of the waxing moon was visible. Gem-
ini, Taurus, and Canis Major all looped around Orion, whom
the Milky Way cradled in one arm. I dumped the ice on the
ground by my steps.

R.H. hollered, "Hey!"

I walked across the road to where R.H. stood, behind the
fence of the exercise yard. On the far side of the yard, detainees
were lined up hip to hip. They walked slowly backward while
combing the sand with their fingers. The boy was in the middle
of the line. I watched him stand up to examine a rock that he'd
discovered. He held it close to his face while turning it over.

"What'd you find out?" R.H. asked.

"Nothing," I said.

"Nothing?"

I didn't think it was worth explaining my theory, aliens had sent the black box to earth as a listening de and the boy had just happened to stumble across it.

"I'm gonna have to bring him in," R.H. said.

This meant that the boy would be interrogated, which, I believed, would yield no useful information, which would then land the boy in solitary while the crying baby tape played over and over.

"Give me another day," I said.

"A whole day?" R.H. said.

"All right, noon tomorrow."

A whistle sounded down the road. I turned to find Spot looking my way while holding the door to the briefing hut open. Light poured out the door, casting Spot's shadow across the road and over the sand dunes beyond.

"You guys going out tonight?" R.H. asked.

"I guess so."

"Where?"

"Hit," I said, without knowing for sure. It just felt that way.

O. Positive kicked open the door to the Facility, and emerged with a bucket. He dumped black water with silver bubbles on the ground, releasing the smell of lavender.

"Hey!" R.H. called to him through the chain link.

O.P. slid off a headphone and raised his eyebrows.

, up the NO VACANCY sign," R.H. said. "They're
ack to Hit."

AGED BULB, the kind you'd hang off the hood of your car
nile doing a tune-up, lit the briefing hut. We sat under the
night on rows of wooden benches. A white bedsheet, which
functioned as our projector screen, hung at the front of the
room. J.J. turned on the projector, squinted against the light.
"We're going back to Heet," he said, using the Iraqi pronun-
ciation for Hit. Then he talked us through the slide show.

The helicopters would drop us off at the train station
around midnight. From there we'd walk across the tracks and
toward the Euphrates on a perpendicular road. We'd take a
right this time. Our target was a four-story building on a corner. Actions on target, or those steps taken to kill or capture
our enemies within, were standard. We'd pull detainees, as
necessary, and exfil southeast. Now J.J. pointed his laser off
the bedsheet, circling a spot on the plywood wall beyond.
Out there we'd find an area with no tank traps, sinkholes, or
barbed wire, where the helos could safely touch down. The
last slide said, simply, QUESTIONS. There were none.

J.J. closed the brief, and white light projected onto the
bedsheet. Spot stood up in that light, his lower lip packed
with chew. He spit into a paper cup and said, "All right. How
to put this?"

Events of the last mission had convinced him that things
were getting a little too loose. Not just with laser discipline,

although dudes were lighting up every moth and bu▓
bit in the shadows, and not only with bullshit on the r▓
case in point, last night's reading of *War and Peace* over t▓
common—but with ACTIONS ON TARGET. With ▓
BREAD AND FUCKIN' BUTTER. And although he shouldn▓
have to reiterate our philosophy, he felt the need. "Speed and
violence," he said. And we allowed him to say it again.

How many times had his ass and the asses of others been
saved by those two elements working in concert? The answer
was unknown and unknowable. We knew that. As the reign-
ing world champions of speed and violence, we knew. So to
go in doing one thing without the other, or neither, or to go in
half-assed? Jesus.

Dust motes followed Spot as he paced in the light of the
projector beam. Nicotine entered his bloodstream through
the thinnest of membranes on the inside of his lip. His wayward eye was humming.

These people, Spot would have us know, were trying to
kill us. Example: Habbaniyah. Example: Ramadi. Example:
Al Qa'im. Goddamn Qa'im in particular, with its remnants of
the Republican Guard. Imagine had we not reacted like unconscious banshees there? Imagine if zero shits and zero fucks
had not been given?

Spot savored a fresh influx of nicotine, affording us time
to imagine what we'd reflexively survived at Qa'im. Which, I
tried.

I really did.

Backmask

Hit, Iraq

Iraqis stuffed rags, blankets, and foam rubber in their windows to protect against who knows what. Heat, perhaps, or noise. Maybe light. We got in regardless.

In a corner room on the second floor of a three-story building in northwest Hit, I backed into a queen-sized roll of foam rubber poking out a window. The window's sash pinched the roll in the middle, leaving half of the foam extending out over the courtyard behind the house, with the other half protruding into the room. I hadn't noticed the foam when I'd entered the darkened room. Now it appeared to me on night vision as that which was not space. Across from it, four feathers sat against a wall, having sorted themselves by age.

"Feathers" was our code word for women. These four may have been a grandmother, a mother, and two daughters. We'd broken into their house looking for the cameraman who'd filmed the executions of Iraqi police officers. We'd ex-

pected to find the cameraman, of whom we had a bi.
ital image, asleep in his bed. Instead, we'd found the fe.
I'd also found a military-aged male, maybe sixteen years
hiding in a third-floor closet. After we'd declared the hou
secure, we'd corralled the feathers into this corner room. I'c
been sent downstairs to guard them.

The grandmother whispered prayers. The mother rocked
from side to side. The oldest daughter had a cleft palate. The
younger girl asked me, "Why are you here?"

Her eyes appeared blank on night vision, but I felt her
stare on me well enough. She wanted me to explain my presence in that room. Or, maybe, she wanted to know why, of all
the houses in Hit, we'd chosen to raid hers. I didn't know
how to explain in English, let alone in Arabic, that it had
come down to the toss of a coin. Heads was this house, tails
the other.

"Why are you here?" she asked again.

"Shh," I tried.

"But why?"

"Be quiet, dear," said the grandmother.

A thump sounded through the ceiling.

"What was that?" asked the older daughter.

I'd found the young man hiding in a closet in the room
directly above us. Actually, I'd found the young man's phone,
which he'd held while squeezing his knees to his chest in the
dark. As the troop's technician, this was my job during the
assault phase: finding phones using a passive homing device.

...d picked the lock on the front door and we'd snuck

...'d followed the phone's signal up the stairs to the

...floor. I'd chased the signal down the hall and into a

...room. I'd homed in on the closet and pointed. Two SEALs,

...sa-Zsa and Mike, had pulled the young man out.

Having analyzed the execution videos, I had an idea of what the cameraman looked like. The boy was too young and squat. Furthermore, I knew what make and model phone the cameraman had used, and the boy's phone didn't match. Nor did it have any evidence in memory of having communicated with the phone in question. Following procedure, I lifted the boy's fingerprints, digitally, then searched for their match in our database. The results came back negative.

The boy would be interrogated, regardless. Zsa-Zsa cuffed him, stood him in a corner, and told him not to move. The thump we'd heard was probably the beginning of his interrogation. It was probably his knees hitting the floor.

Through the ceiling, I heard the boy say, "Please."

"That's Saif," said the mother.

"Impossible," said the grandmother. "Saif is in Baghdad."

"He sounds far away," said the older daughter.

The mother held the grandmother's hand. "Mama, you're thinking of Ali. *Ali* is in Baghdad."

"Be quiet," I said to all of them, in Arabic.

Back at our outpost, in the plywood hut where we dressed for missions, a list of Arabic phrases hung on the wall. Thumbing rounds into a magazine, I'd study that list: the

words for "hands up," "tell the truth," "everybody
cetera. The only phrase I could remember, though, w
one for "be quiet." Probably because every night th
walked across the moonlit desert, or crept through the b
streets of Hit, or crouched while getting into position for a
raid, I felt like I was making too much noise. My knees
cracked, my breath rattled, my ears rang. I'd stop breathing
and not move a muscle, yet I couldn't keep my thoughts from
jangling.

"You speak Arabic?" asked the younger girl.

"No," I answered, in English. I understood Arabic, however, if I paid attention. It was like listening to Zeppelin backward.

I'd first heard the rumors about Zeppelin's satanic mes-
sages back in 1981, when I was in the eighth grade. Jimmy
Page, the lead guitarist of the band, had made a deal with the
devil in exchange for fame. Satan himself had woven a backward message into the lyrics of "Stairway to Heaven." Expo-
sure to that message turned listeners into disciples of the
Antichrist. I hadn't necessarily believed all that, but I'd
wanted to hear the message for myself. So, one day I put *Led
Zeppelin IV* on the turntable. I found the lyrics in question,
shifted the turntable into neutral, and, with my index finger
on the label, spun the record in reverse. It took a while to get
the speed just right, so that something like a voice creaked
out of the speakers. The voice that emerged, however, sounded
more like that of a regular person than Satan. But a regular

a parallel world who, upon finding a door to ours,
anaged to crack it open long enough to say a few
s. Having tuned my ear to that frequency, I was able to
erstand the feathers.

I understood the dogs in the same way. Packs of wild dogs
roamed the deserts of Iraq. I'd see them while sitting in the
door of the Black Hawk, next to the cannon, during our long
rides out into the night. We'd fly over rolling sand dunes of
uniform amplitude, frequency, and moon shadow as the dogs
ran in wedge-shaped packs below. The gunner would lead
them while test-firing the cannon.

The muzzle's heart-shaped flame would warm my cheek.
Tracers would bend down toward the running dogs, who,
leaving their dead behind, would take off in a new direction.
We'd touch down in the sand, far from anything. I'd step out
the door, my legs half-asleep. The lifting Black Hawk would
raise the sand into suspension, creating a golden haze on
night vision. Off goggles it'd be pitch-black. I'd wait for
the sand to settle, and for my teammates to emerge from the
haze. Then I'd fall into formation for our walk across the
desert toward Hit, Ramadi, or Fallujah. Along the way, dogs
would swoop in from distant sand dunes. They'd climb out of
deep, twisting wadis. They'd leap straight out of the pitch-
black nothing. And they'd start talking.

The dogs would appear white-hot on night vision. Blue
static would crackle in their fur. To the naked eye, they'd look
jet-black and oily. Sneezing and baring their teeth, they'd trot

alongside us. Earlier that night, as we'd patrolled eas
across the desert toward Hit, one dog had chosen to fo.
me. When I'd sped up, it had sped up. When I'd stopped
rest, it had stopped, too. During one such respite, the dog hac
looked at me, and said, "Sometimes sedition, sometimes
blight."

Months later, after I returned home, I looked up "sedition." I also looked up a poem by Rudyard Kipling called
"Boots," which the dogs liked to recite when covering large
distances.

Kipling's poem is about a British soldier in Africa during
the Second Boer War who, as a member of an infantry regi-
ment, endures a forced march across eight hundred miles of
hot, shifting sands. The days and weeks spent marching are
compressed into lines and stanzas. At the outset of the poem,
the soldier seems resigned to his lot. The dogs in Iraq, therefore, chant in time with the march: *Boots! Boots! Movin' up
and down again!* Then the miles begin to take their toll on the
soldier. His heart knocks like a tiny fist; his head throbs under
the hammering sun. Day after day, all he sees are the boots of
the men marching in front of him. Boots rising and falling.
Boots kicking up sand. Boots disappearing and reappearing
in a gritty haze. The sight eventually drives the soldier insane.
So, by the end of the poem, either the dogs are telepathic or
it's just my imagination whispering, *Boots.*

I listened for those dogs through the window propped
open by the roll of foam rubber while starlight squeezed into

m. It spilled out the doorway and into the hall. Faint
ds of an orderly, if unproductive, search arrived from the
ounding darkness—a dresser drawer sliding open, a
oset hinge squeaking. Someone tapped a finger against a
wall, hunting for voids. We'd been inside that house for thirty
minutes, and if we hadn't found anything yet, we weren't
going to.

Tull, on his way upstairs, passed the door to the room
where I was guarding the feathers. I followed him into the
hall.

"Hey," I said.

Tull turned around. His beard looked like a wood carving
of a beard. "Yeah?" he asked.

"Tell Zsa-Zsa to ask the kid about Ali," I said.

"Who the fuck's Ali?"

"They're talking about him in there," I said, thumbing
back toward the feathers. "I think he's the kid's brother. But
he could also be our cameraman."

Tull nodded and continued down the hall. I returned to
guard the feathers.

"Ali is upstairs, asleep in bed," the grandmother told me
when I walked into the room.

"No, Mama," the mother said. "Ali is with his family in
Baghdad."

"Why are you here?" the older daughter asked me.

It was almost one A.M. on a Saturday. The insurgents'
grim campaign against the Iraqi police had begun the previ-

ous Wednesday. That morning, six cops had vanished their station in northeast Hit. That night, their bodies been found in the bitumen mines north of Hit. Thursd. morning, insurgents had posted the first video online.

That video showed six cops, blindfolded and kneeling at the edge of a pit, as a hooded gunman went down the line, shooting each man in the back of the head. Our analysts had traced the video's origins to an Internet café in the south end of town. We'd broken into that café on Thursday night.

The café was the size of a broom closet. Two computers were jammed atop a school desk inside. I'd sat in a little kid's chair. The ghost drive I'd used to copy all the files had chirped like a sparrow at a birdbath. It had whirred like that same sparrow shaking water off its back. The download had taken a lot longer than I'd thought. Meanwhile, the dogs, waiting for us on the edge of town, had remained silent.

Back at the outpost, early Friday morning, I'd sifted through the files that I'd ghosted from the café. I'd found the original file of the first video. Then I'd searched for other videos taken by the same phone, ones that had been downloaded onto the café computer but not uploaded onto the Web. That was how I'd found the second video—recorded on Thursday morning, according to the time stamp—which appeared to show the execution of a seventh cop.

The second video begins in the cop's kitchen as the insurgents struggle to remove him from his breakfast table. I counted four insurgents including the cameraman, who, it d, had inadvertently begun recording during the melee. of the scene in the kitchen is a blur, except for a brief k at an oval of flatbread on a green plate and a peek at eam rising from a coffeepot on the stove. "Fuck your sister," the cop says, seemingly through his teeth. Next comes a long stare at a puddle of milk on the kitchen's linoleum floor, accompanied by sounds of the cop choking. Then everybody files out the back door.

Brick stairs descend into a brick courtyard. The cameraman almost shuts the camera off, thinking he needs to turn it on, but it's already recording. Realizing his mistake, he says, "Shit!"

The cameraman focuses on the seventh cop, breathing hard and bleeding from his nose. He's kneeling before a thick vine, heavy with blue flowers. An insurgent, at the edge of the landscape frame, holds up something for the cop to read. The cameraman zooms in on the cop's face. The cop's green eyes scan the text. "Out loud," the insurgent tells him. The cop looks directly at the camera, and says, "Here I am in my little garden with morning glories."

The cameraman drops the phone, and it lands lens down on the bricks. The resulting darkness is maroon. A pistol fires. Shoes scuffle. "You missed it!" says one of the insurgents. "Fuck me," the cameraman says, picking up the phone. It records a split second of morning glories creeping over a wall, then a tall cloud, in the background, tinted pink by the sunrise. The cameraman shoves the phone into his pocket

while it's still recording. The video goes dark again.
audio continues, though, with sounds of the cameraman ru[n]-
ning behind the other insurgents—into the kitchen, throug[h]
the house, and out the front door. A getaway car idles roughly.
The cameraman climbs in. Doors slam, and the insurgents
drive away.

Gears grind and brakes squeal. The insurgents drive for
less than a minute, without talking, before they come to a
puttering stop. The cameraman gets out. "Peace," he says to
the others, and the car door closes behind him.

The cameraman's brothers-in-arms drive away, shifting
into second, then third. The cameraman, I imagine, must've
watched them go. He must've wished that he'd had the chance
to explain what had happened, back there, with the camera.
He must've wanted to hear his comrades say that it would be
fine, that there'd be other chances. During the getaway, the
cameraman would've watched them closely for signs of lost
trust. Perhaps they'd shown no signs, they just wouldn't return. While the cameraman considers this, the audio features
static. Then a gate with a metal latch opens and closes. The
cameraman removes his phone from his pocket. There's a
flash of him with the rising sun in the background; then the
image steadies on a patch of hard dirt. The cameraman real-
izes that he's been recording this whole time. "Fuck me," he
says again, and the video ends.

Rewinding just five seconds, to the part before the patch
of hard dirt, where the cameraman's silhouette flashed, I'd

...vered a cellphone tower standing behind him. Intel ...nd five such towers in Hit. Knowing the height of those ...wers and the position of the sun in the sky at that time of ...day, they were able to triangulate five possible locations for the cameraman. Cross-referencing those locations onto satellite imagery, they'd discovered that two of them were in gated courtyards with dirt surfaces. Zsa-Zsa had flipped the coin to decide which one we'd go to. I'd called heads as it ascended.

It appeared, however, that I should've called tails. The feathers, I'm sure, would've agreed. But they no longer seemed to care why I was there. They just wanted me and the rest of the troop to leave, thereby returning their house and their lives to them.

Tull passed the open door going the other way, followed by Zsa-Zsa, who stuck his head into the room.

"Last man," Zsa-Zsa said to me.

I told the feathers to stay, in English; then I pointed at my watch and held up ten fingers. They gave me blank looks. I held my hand out, like, *Stay*. The mother nodded and patted the grandmother's leg. The older daughter explained what I meant to the younger: Stay put for ten minutes. I followed Zsa-Zsa out of the room and down the stairs.

The living room's velvet curtains conjured disgraced royalty. The grease stains on the kitchen walls resembled Rorschach tests. I exited through the back door, into the courtyard, to find the troop filing through the gate into the

alley. They were turning east, away from the desert and c
rendezvous with the helicopters.

I walked over to Tull, who was standing where the cameraman would've been at the moment he realized that his
phone had recorded the entire getaway.

"Are we going to the other place?" I whispered.

"Yeah," Tull said.

The troop continued to pass through the gate. Dogs
streamed by, following my brothers down the alley. A skinny
mongrel lingered for me outside the gate. I waited until everybody else was gone.

I turned to look up at the window with its roll of foam
rubber sticking out, and there I saw the youngest feather. Her
forehead was pressed against the glass.

I imagined that the older sister asked, "Are they gone?"

The youngest feather stared at me, staring back.

"Not yet," she said.

Acknowledgments

———

Thanks—

To my wife, Alaina—everyone else is loco. To Betta and Eli: someday you will look upon new and improved versions of yourselves and you will be at an equal loss for words. To brother Jon, with whom I share both heart and mind. To Mom, Dad, and sister Amy, for your love and support. To George Saunders, whose fiction class I took on a whim, and who turned it into my life's work. To Andy Ward, my patient friend, for always listening. To Esther and Liz, for showing me the ropes. And to Karen Karbo, for your generous guidance.

To Deborah Treisman: when the vertical bars of blue light talk, it's in your voice.

To those who provide indispensable shelter, knowledge, and encouragement for rejects of all shapes and sizes: Summer Literary Seminars, *Tin House,* the Lannan Foundation.

To rejects of all shapes and sizes.

And last but not least, a sacred debt to the men and women of Naval Special Warfare Development Group.

WILL MACKIN is a veteran of the U.S. Navy. His writing has appeared in *The New Yorker, GQ, The New York Times Magazine,* and *The Best American Short Stories 2014.* A native of New Jersey, he currently lives in New Mexico. *Bring Out the Dog* is his first book.

wmackin.com

Printed in the United States
by Baker & Taylor Publisher Services